The Complete Woman

M.L. Lexi

"The Complete Woman" Edition

Published by M.L. Lexi

Cover design by M.L. Lexi.

ISBN: 978-1-7752956-5-5

Visit our website at www.mllexi.com

Visit our blog at mllexi.blog

Also by M.L. Lexi

THE GUILTY WOMAN

Coming Soon

THE DETERMINED WOMAN

THE FORGIVING WOMAN

THE NOBLE WOMAN

THE UNFAITHFUL WOMAN

For Albert,

who has made this journey through life a memorable one.

And to my family, here and long gone,

who have made me who I am today.

Love can pierce our darkest moments pouring light and hope

into our sad existence.

—M.L. Lexi

The Complete Woman

One

Vanessa - December 1969

THE ANXIETY THAT had stabbed at the center of Natalia's chest since getting the phone call amplified tenfold as she rushed past the ambulance in the emergency bay. Lights rotating like a beacon in the night, the paramedics unloaded the man gasping deeply for oxygen his injured body starved for between moans of pain. He was middle-aged, with peppered hair mussed around an aging face, creased with the roadmap of life. The sheet that cocooned him was stained red.

Natalia felt her stomach turn, and the bile rise to her throat.

Swallow. Swallow. Swallow.

She wondered how the two guarding police officers flanking the ambulance were able to stand there with an expression of absolute indifference as the paramedics wheeled the man off.

For one heady moment she thought that could have been Vanessa, and the sick ball at the pit of her stomach tightened. She breathed for calm, once, twice. As composed as she could manage to get, Natalia made her way past the unmarked police cars, the gawkers, cameras and flashbulbs through the sliding doors. Bulleting past the emergency waiting room, she made a dash for the nursing station.

"I'm looking for someone who was brought in by ambulance an hour ago," Natalia said to the woman behind the desk when the mast of flaming red hair rose. Her vibrant blue eyes, set in a face speckled with freckles, were far chipper than Natalia expected.

Behind Natalia, the soft moans from an elderly woman in a wheelchair, her hand tightly pressed to her chest, mingled with the assuring words from her kneeling daughter. A mother in examination room A rocked her baby in her arms as fatigued eyes begging for sleep looked down in worry. One room over, a man gently patted his wife on the back when she tried to regain breath after the coughing bout she'd just endured. In the distance, the wail of an incoming ambulance got louder and louder as it neared the emergency bay.

"What's the patient's name?" Red asked.

"Vanessa Roberts," Natalia said.

Red tapped a pencil on the clipboard as she scanned it. "Just a moment, please. I need to check with her nurse," she said, turning to the plump brunette in the blinding white, uniform at the end of the counter. "Margie, do you know if Roberts has been taken up to ICU yet?"

Natalia's heart took one hard leap into her throat. "ICU? Why is she being taken to ICU?"

Setting pencil and clipboard down, Red swiveled back to Natalia, and shot a sidelong glance in her direction. "Are you family?"

"I'm her sister," Natalia nervously stammered, and Red cocked a dubious brow. "I need to see her, please. I need to make sure she's okay."

The questioning brow still raised Red said, "Let me see what I can do."

After a short, one-sided telephone conversation with the head nurse in ICU, Red hung up and looked up at Natalia. "You can go upstairs to the ICU waiting room. Take the elevator down the hall to the eighteenth floor."

"Do you know which doctor is looking after her?" Natalia's voice trembled.

"Dr. Steward. She's one of our best neurologists. Your sister is in good hands," Red said.

The thump of panic reached deep into Natalia's chest. "Neurologist?"

"Our best, and they'll answer all your questions upstairs."

Natalia managed an appreciative smile, and made her way to the bank of elevators where she boarded the first one to ping. Pressing the designated floor, she watched the numbers above her light up—fifteen…sixteen…seventeen—at an alarming slow pace. The ride felt interminable.

The moment the elevator doors slid open on the eighteenth floor, Natalia came face to face with the worried look on the slate gray eyes that magnified every thought in her head. "How is she, Tom? Have you seen her? What happened? Why is she here?"

Tom's raven black, thick hair looked as if it had seen a few too many rakes of his fingers. "No, I haven't seen or know how she is. They told me to wait here for the doctor. That was an hour ago." His tall, slender body hunched as he exchanged an anxious look with Natalia.

"Why don't we head into the waiting room?" Tom asked.

"Sure, fine. Lead the way." Natalia followed him into the waiting room although she sensed that sitting and waiting was the last thing he wanted to do. It was the last thing she wanted to do.

The room was small and devoid of human life. Walls were washed in white, and gray carpeting lay at their feet. A black framed clock marking the hour of ten thirty p.m. hung on one wall and a framed colorful print—the only semblance of color in the drab room—of an Italian promenade on the other. A muted television sitting on a shelf in one corner played the words, "I'm loving it," and below it, a square wood table held an assortment of weathered magazines. The wide unblinded window overlooked a sparsely trafficked University Avenue blanketed in snow.

Natalia took a seat in one of the padded green chairs lined against the wall, and Tom followed suit and sank his long frame into the chair next to her. The familiar hospital stench of antiseptic, despair, and sickness seeped deep into Natalia like the tentacles of a stinging jellyfish.

"Why is she up here? Why the ICU, Tom?" She kept her anxious eyes direct on him.

He pressed his fingers to his eyes; his handsome face brimmed with worry. "I was in the emergency room with her for a while. We were talking. She was alert, coherent, and then out of nowhere she went into a seizure. The doctors and nurses swarmed her bed, and after several minutes managed to stabilize her. She seemed fine for a half hour or so. We spoke at length. She was giving me instructions. I'm her solicitor, and the only one here," he said when Natalia's brows creased. "I was holding her hand when she began to grip it tighter and tighter."

He remained silent for a moment, swallowing hard. "Then she released her hold of my hand and began to convulse again, this time more violently. They called a code blue and the medical team sprinted to her bed. I heard instructions, and unintelligible codes called out. Who the hell knew what they were saying." In a gesture of pure frustration, he dragged a hand through his hair.

"After twenty-five minutes of watching this unfold before me, I watched her wheeled past me. She was so…pale, so…lifeless." Tom stopped for breath. "They told me they were transferring her to the ICU. They told me to wait here, that they would be out to update me as soon as they could. That was eons ago."

The shudder of fear working up her spine, Natalia reached for Tom's hand. "She'll be fine, Tom. She'll be just fine. She's stronger than any of us," she said in the most reassuring tone she could muster.

The tears spilling hot, Natalia's eyes drifted to the swirling snow outside the window and let her mind drift back in time.

Two

Four Years Earlier

FINDING YOUR TRUE love is life's destiny. It's as essential as the oxygen we breathe. It's the Holy Grail that we search for all of our lives. Yet few of us are fortunate enough to find it.

For years, I searched for the type of unconditional love that echoes through eternity, gives without reservation, makes no demands, or judgment, and expects nothing in return. That type of love, I learned, is a rare find. So rare that there are those who scoff at the mere idea that it even exists.

I was one of those skeptics—until I met Paxton Reed.

My name is Natalia Rossi, and I was twenty-seven years old when fate brought Pax into my life. I believed it was fate, because ours was a chance meeting written in the stars.

IN THE DISTANCE, A JULY SUN slipped into its nightly slumber, and a bone-white moon rose and rode over the still waters of Lake Ontario. The scent of lilac and jasmine mingled in the air, and I could hear the faint sound of waves lapping the shore as I made my way along the planked boardwalk.

I loved the Beaches. The area in the southeast end of Toronto felt more like a lakeside resort town than a big city neighborhood. In the summertime, thousands of Torontonians and tourists flocked to the area to take lakeside strolls along the beautiful two-mile boardwalk, or feel sun-bleached sand sliding between their toes on the stretch of beach, or to dine and shop at the eclectic restaurants and stores.

There was always something going on, and tonight the Beaches was out in full for the International Music Festival. The twelve-block stretch of Queen Street closed off to traffic between Woodbine and Beech Avenue was packed with music enthusiasts who flocked to enjoy the mellow harmonies of the dozens of performing bands or simply soak in the vibrant street scene.

Scents of lake, early summer, and barbecued meats lingered in the air. Music flowed from amplifiers as couples strolled at a leisure pace. Children dashed from vendor to vendor eyeing the sweets and food on display deciding what they wanted to eat next. A group of people joined in excited laughter and encouragement when a young girl broke into dance when a band named DA Band launched into their rendition of the twist.

I arrived alone, but soon after met up with a group of friends at The Bistro, a quaint Italian restaurant with flagstone-tiled floor, dark walnut tables, friendly staff, and excellent food. The Bistro was where we got together for dinner as often as our busy lives allowed. Vanessa and her date were already there, as was the rest of the group. The nine of us—nine because I was always the uncoupled one—

were ushered to our usual table by the window, overlooking Queen Street. I took the seat next to Vanessa, my best friend since elementary school. Although tonight I wasn't so sure she was going to bother much with me. Vanessa's date—or, in her words, "the flavor of the week"—a doe-eyed, tanned Adonis with smoky dark hair who looked as if he'd stepped off the cover of GQ, couldn't keep his eyes off her. And she couldn't keep hers off him.

Introductions made, Tom Webster took his eyes off Vanessa long enough to gaze up at the man who walked up to our table.

"Hey, Pax, glad you could make it. This is Vanessa Roberts and that's Nata…"

"Natalia, Natalia Rossi," Vanessa jumped in to the rescue when Adonis' brain, in the wake of her flirtatious coded eye messages, went numb.

Tom's eyes rolled to the back of his head as Vanessa whispered in his ear. He absentmindedly waved a hand in the air and said, "Grab a seat, Pax." Whether Pax did or did not was clearly of no consequence to him.

Pax looked my way and flashed a quick, stunning smile that left me staring at him. His eyes were as blue as a calm ocean, and at that moment, I'd say mine were a tempestuous sea green. He was leanly built, the sinewy arms beneath crisp white silk unmistakable. His hair was black as a midnight sky, thick and wavy, and his jaw, sharp as a knife's blade, bore a fashionable stubble that I though sensual. I'd put him at over six feet, and although he wasn't as model gorgeous as Mr. Adonis, he was a looker with a smoldering sexuality that made my heart take one hard leap into my throat.

I suddenly felt conscious of my simple appearance and prayed to God that at the least my crimson pout was on right and my chestnut curls weren't in a disheveled mess.

"Let's do the introductions properly. I'm Paxton Reed. My friends call me Pax," he said with an outstretched hand.

I met his smile and reached for the offered hand. It was warm and strong, and left me wanting to hold it forever.

"I'm Natalia Rossi." The scent of soap and man slid in to me. My stomach muscles tightened and my mind roved with thoughts it hadn't seen for some time.

"Do you mind if I sit here?" His gaze didn't waver, and when I nodded— admittedly more eagerly than I should have—he eased his six-foot frame into the seat next to me.

My heart took a hard leap into my throat, and not trusting my voice, I motioned for everyone at the table to introduce themselves.

"Please excuse Tom. This is the way he gets when he's in love," Pax said with a smile that lit up the room.

"Her too," I mumbled, eyeing Vanessa with envy. Ever since I could remember, men flocked to her in a zombie-like state, falling head over heels from the moment they set eyes on her.

I never had such luck. Meeting men didn't come easily to me, and talking to them was a skill I had yet to master in my late twenties. I didn't know how to bat my eyelashes or be coy, or bring the tone of my voice down to that sensual level that made men lean in closer to you. Never trusting my voice or what my brain might compel me to say around the opposite sex, I often resorted to the best option available— silence.

Pax offered to buy me a glass of wine, and desperately needing the infusion of alcohol, I accepted. I was happy when he ordered a bottle. Halfway through my first glass, the wine having wound its way through my system, I felt more at ease. By the start of my second glass, the knot of tension in my stomach relaxed and I began to chat up a storm. Alcohol always had that effect on me, although Pax was easy going, and made conversing easy. We spent the rest of the night talking about anything and everything.

I learned that Pax was three years older than I was. That he and Tom, having met first year of university, were recruited straight out of law school by Roth & Associates, one of the top legal firms in the country. Pax, alongside Tom, practiced municipal and planning law, although Tom was making the jump to the more lucrative field of family law. I learned that Pax, an only child, had recently moved back to his childhood home to care for his ill, widowed mother.

I told Pax as much as I could about myself, including that I was a second-grade teacher at St. Mary's Elementary, and that I loved my job and my children. I let out an alcohol-infused giggle when his eyes opened wide, and I explained that I referred to my students as my children.

"Why don't you ask Pax to accompany you to your parents' wedding anniversary this weekend instead of taking me as your plus one, Natalia?" Vanessa let her eyebrows rise above persuading eyes when she jumped into our conversation.

"I…um…ah…" I thought silence fit best after my eloquent stammer, and I closed my mouth.

Vanessa waited a beat before turning to Pax. "Pick Natalia up Saturday, at noon." She reached into Tom's jacket pocket for his pen, and proceeded to write down the address on a cocktail napkin.

"Are you always this direct?" Pax asked Vanessa. I wished I could slither off my chair and hide under the table.

"The lady always speaks her mind." Tom winked. "Don't you, darling?"

"Many like that about me. You do don't you, baby?" Vanessa said to Tom with a flutter of her inky lashes.

"Jesus," I said feeling the flush of heat on my chest rise to my cheeks.

Vanessa handed Pax the napkin with the address and directions. "The reception is at her parents' home on the Bridle Path. It's black tie, and her mother is a persnickety sort, so make sure to pretty yourself up."

"Please ignore her. You don't need to escort me anywhere,"

Pax tucked the napkin into his jacket pocket. "But I'd like to. It sounds like fun."

Delight rippled through me at his response, but I only managed a simple, "All right."

THE LAST ONES LEFT AT OUR table, Pax and I closed the restaurant down. When we walked outside, expecting to part ways, I said, "Good night," and started toward my car.

That's when Pax surprised me with, "Can I walk you to your car?" and I felt the pinch of joy at the center of my stomach.

"I'm just over there," I said titillated by the thought that the evening wasn't about to end there and then.

Under a black canopy twinkling with the light of a thousand stars and with a warm wind blowing leisurely, Pax made the one-block walk with me. The streets were now almost empty, and the cacophony of sounds that had filled them earlier in the night had died down to a dull hum.

The walk to my car was far too short. Once there, we simply stood facing each other in a comfortable silence. The light from a street lamp cast a cone shaped glow around us and somewhere cicadas were crying out for love. From the corner of my eye, I caught sight of a shooting star, and I made a wish. As the trail of light faded into the darkness, Pax trailed a fingertip along my cheek sending shockwaves through me that made me tingle all over.

My wish coming true he whispered, "I'd love to kiss you."

With the thrill of anticipation pounding under my skin, I eased forward. His blue eyes deepened as he leaned down to my five-foot-six-inch height and eagerly took my mouth. His lips were warm and soft and the taste of wine on them exploded inside me, flowed through me strong and steady like a river with no end.

Our lips met for a brief few seconds. He wasn't the first man I'd kissed, but his kiss was the most memorable of my twenty-seven-year existence.

My heartbeat still thundered in my ears when I pulled out of the parking lot, and watching him through my rearview mirror, I decided that he was the man I was going to marry.

Three

PAX SEEMED FRAZZLED, but in control when we stepped into my parents' Amazon-sized backyard. Guests, numbering in the hundreds, milled on the terrace, at the two bars at opposite ends of the pool, around the fountain where foot-long carp swam, and throughout the manicured gardens. There were three large tents. Ice sculptures carved in the shape of the number thirty with flowing Dom Pérignon welcomed guests at the entrance of each. At the center of round tables draped in white linen, and chairs covered in matte-gold, birds of paradise—my mother's favourite—speared out of bronze vases. The lazy scent of lilac and linden blossoms drifted in the air.

"Wow!" Pax's daunting sigh was masked by burst of birdsong that broke from the canopy of green foliage above us.

"Wow indeed. I should have warned you. My mother has a tendency to only do the wow!"

"This is quite…"

"Ostentatious? Way over the top?"

"I was thinking more along the lines of…" He dug his hands into his pockets, "Intimidating. So, this is where you grew up?"

"Not until my early teens when dad teamed up with his partner and he secured his first high-rise construction deal."

"Wait, Rossi." Blue eyes as clear as glass fixed wide in shock and stared at me. "Jesus, your father is Rob Rossi the real estate developer with condos, and homes, and commercial buildings all across the country?"

I nodded. "It's not as big a deal as…"

"That's a huge deal. I…"

"Who's your friend, Natalia?" Caterina's voice came at us from behind in her customary icy tone. Bronzed skin against white Armani silk, her blonde perfectly coiffed waves spilled over her bare shoulders made her look summery and youthful.

"Pax Reed, Caterina Stanton, my sister."

"Pleasure to meet you." Pax held out a hand for hers and she met it.

"The pleasure is all mine." Her diamond-studded hand lifted to her throat, and traced fingers over the even larger diamond at the end of the gold chain. "You a new friend of Natalia's? I don't believe I've seen you before." Caterina eyed him with predatory eyes.

"You haven't met Pax before." I jumped in before Pax could answer.

"I thought so. I'd remember you. Those blue eyes and that smoldering sexuality would be hard to forget." She playfully twisted a strand of hair around her finger.

"Ummm…thank you?" Pax's tone betrayed his uneasiness and I could see my sister taking pleasure in it.

"You're very welcome," she whispered in a breathy voice.

"Blake and Diana just walked in, Caterina. You should go greet your in-laws," I said to distract from the awkward moment. Making people ill at east was my sister's specialty.

"Stanton...your in-laws are Blake and Diana Stanton?" Pax's eyes flashed an astonished look.

"Yes, they are." The eyes beneath the perfectly shaped brows beamed with pride. If there was one thing Caterina enjoyed was flaunting the Stanton name. It was the only reason, I believed, she had married Michael Stanton. "Would you like an introduction?"

"No, no thank you. I just..."

"Wanted to know who the players are," Caterina finished for Pax. "See that distinguished looking group of men over there? That's William Weston, founder of the multi-million dollar William Weston Ltd. The man next to him is Steve Rogers the communications giant. Well, you get the idea. Their combined wealth is in the billions," she said with a note of self-importance, as we watched the men nod to one another in what looked more like collection of bobble-heads than powerful tycoons.

"Why don't you grab us a drink at the bar?" I asked Pax, deciding that what he needed was distance from my sister who could have gone on forever.

"What my sister is saying is that you better get away from me before I sink my claws into you. Isn't that right, dear sister?"

"I'll have a Cosmo, Pax, and she doesn't need a drink," I said when Caterina started to open her mouth.

"I guess you won't be getting me one, handsome. She's been a killjoy since we were children." Caterina followed Pax's tight behind when he walked away. "He's cute, and not just because he has that sexy James Bond look going for him in that black tuxedo. I wonder how good he is in bed."

"Jesus, Caterina, you're a married woman now. You have been for three years. Do you still need to come on to every man you meet?"

"Oh, ease up. I'm married, but I'm not dead. It's all in good fun."

"He's my date."

Caterina's eyes lifted above the rim of her sunglasses. "You're in love with him."

My heart tripped at the comment, and without regard for my brain, my mouth shot out in defense, "I'm not. How could I be, I barely know him? He's a…friend. That's all he is."

"You are. I thought he was a fun roll in the sheets for you, but you're in love with simple, handsome Pax."

"When have you known me to go out with someone just for 'a roll in the sheets' as you so crudely put it. And don't call him simple."

"He is simple and completely out of his depth here. That's a fact, Natalia. You know that. What does he do?"

I told her.

"Hmmm, well, lawyer or not, you know Mom's going to hate him. I could already hear her. 'Whatever is going on with that boy you stop it now, Natalia. He's not the kind of people we are.'"

"I know, but I don't care."

"Well, whatever he is, it's very brave of you. I know for you it's all about falling in love, making a family, having that brood of children you've dreamed about all of your life, but you well know that's not what mother wants for us. She wants status, a prominent last name, wealth, and what mommy wants, mommy gets." The concerned look on my face prompted her to say. "Don't look so worried, Natalia. If you really want him, you'll fight her as you always do. She can't control you as she can me. It's why the two of you clash like oil and water. Good luck with that."

Caterina started away, her five-inch Ferragamo's sinking into the perfectly manicured green grass.

I CAUGHT SIGHT OF THE WOMAN walking across the terrace, heels clicking on gray slate. She was a diminutive woman, but forceful, and as she made her way toward Pax and me the throngs of guest in her path parted like Moses and the Red Sea.

As was always the case, Rose Adele Rossi was perfectly made up, from the salon-styled hair to the black snakeskin stilettos on her feet. She had an aristocratic nose and high cheekbones that were set in a delicate olive face with skin that was as flawless as the rubies draping her neck. Today she wore a yellow, one-shoulder mermaid dress that highlighted the enviable figure, which at fifty-five, she kept fit through sheer determination.

To say that my mother was an attractive woman was an understatement. Although it didn't come without effort on her part, my mother could sway a room of men to turn in her direction when she sashayed in the seductive way that came so naturally to her. As much as she loved the attention, I suspected she went out of her way to attract roving eyes to keep my father on his toes.

"Hello, dear." She leaned in to give me a peck that stopped inches from my cheek, then proceeded to scan judgmental green eyes over me. "I wished you would have kept the hair appointment I made for you with Angelo and his make-up artist, Monica. But you do love the simple look."

My mother was the epitome of etiquette, propriety, and manners to everyone, but me.

"I think she looks perfect," Pax said to my surprise.

"You do, do you?" Mom turned to Pax and got a nod. "Caterina tells me you're a lawyer Mr. Reed, is it?" Mom said, and I thought, here we go with the layers of husband qualifying questions.

"Mom, please." I said as the band launched into their rendition of The Beatles, Help. Appropriate, I thought.

"Pax, ma'am, and yes I practice municipal and planning law." Pax's voice rose over the din of conversation and laughter overtaking the conversation.

"Caterina also tells me you're not only following in your father's footsteps, but that you're working in his firm. Very admirable for you to want to carry on his legacy." Mom probed in that skillful passive aggressive way honed through years of practice.

The familiar feeling of uneasiness my mother managed to impart on me whenever she was around my dates crept up my spine. "Please, Mom," I pleaded to deaf ears.

"Natalia, what is wrong with me having an interest in your friend's." Mom turned to Pax. "How…"

"Daddy, don't you look handsome." I kissed him on his approach and whispered, "Help," in his ear.

He handed my mother a flute, bubbling with Dom Pérignon. "I'd rather feel comfortable, but no, your mother has to throw a black-tie affair. Are you bothering Natalia and her guest, Rose?"

Mom shot a glare at my father that would have set him aflame.

"Ummm, Daddy, I'd like you to meet Pax Reed. Pax, Rob Rossi."

"Nice to meet you, young man." Daddy exchanged a handshake with Pax then turned to me. "And you, princess, you look the picture of absolute beauty."

"You're only saying that because…"

"Because it's absolutely true."

I leaned into him when he wrapped his arm around me. "Thank you, and happy anniversary. How does it feel to be married for…?"

"Hush, Natalia. Pax here was telling me he's a municipal and planning lawyer, and that he works for his father's law firm." My mother caught my father up.

"You've been misinformed, Mrs. Rossi. I am a lawyer, but I work for Roth & Associates. My father was an assembly line worker. I'm actually the first of my family to go to university. It was of great pride to my family when I graduated top of my class," Pax said simply, and I could feel my mother stiffen beside me.

"An assembly worker?" She pressed a hand to her stomach.

"Should drink some of that Dom, Rose," my father said seemingly taking pleasure in the moment.

My mother swilled Dom too quickly for pleasure, and I thought then that I'd never seen her drink anything that required the shade of a tiny, colorful umbrella.

"As in on-the-line at a manufacturing facility? As in a…a factory?" my mother asked when she'd regained her composure.

Although my mother came from workingmen's roots— her father being a Sicilian sheep farmer—she'd forgotten her humble beginnings long ago. Particularly so when my father partnered with Blake Stanton to form Stanton & Rossi Developments twenty years ago. The Stanton name bore all the qualities my mother greatly admired, a respected name steeped in history, and bred by generations of old Stanton money—oodles of it. When my sister married Blake's son, Michael, three years ago, my mother had officially crossed into blue-blood terrain, and blinded her to her humble past.

"Yes, ma'am. He worked at the General Motors plant. He was a loyal employee for over thirty years. He loved to get his hands dirty, you know like right down into the greasy stuff. I remember him coming home with those blackened hands, and that grease rooted under his nails." The smirk lurking at the corner of Pax's eyes told me his comment was a calculated one.

I gathered my father did too when with a gleam of humor in his eyes, he said, "He sounds like my kind of man, hardworking, reliable and trustworthy. Very much like your father, Rose. Do you remember how your father used to come home with sheep manu—"

With deep inhaled breaths, my mother pressed her hand to her heart. "Rob, I don't believe Pax is interested in hearing our family history," she said unblinking as she gulped the remaining Dom in her glass in one gulp.

"You should be proud of your father, and your roots, son," Daddy said.

Pax met my father's eyes with a full smile. "I am, sir."

"It certainly has been a pleasure meeting you, son. Now, Rose, let's get that glass of yours topped up with something stronger than Dom. I have a suspicion you're in desperate need of a stiffer drink right at this moment." Daddy leaned in to kiss me on the cheek and whispered, "This one's a keeper," then steered my mother toward the furthest bar from us.

In the distance, I caught Caterina's lip twitching.

PAX AND I SPENT THE REST of the night away from the crowds. In the gazebo with the flowering vines trailing from its sides and flanked with red roses, we shared a bottle of wine, and talked and talked. The more I learned about Pax, the more I liked him. With the sound of cicadas and the warm air laced with the scent of summer and blooms all around us, Pax and I watched the rays of sunshine descending between the trees until night fell.

The moon floated near the horizon and shadows moved behind the trees when Pax leaned in and took me into the long, sweet kiss that filled my heart and soul with the love I'd searched for so long. I'd never expected to feel that strong connection with him, that jolt of love, and now it was all I wanted.

Like teenagers in love, we held hands the entire drive home. His thumb tracing the contours of my hand in slow, tender strokes had me debating whether to invite him up for a nightcap. I wished Vanessa were there with us. She would have settled the debate in my head seconds in by blurting out, "Pax, Natalia wants to go a few rounds with you between the sheets. Make sure you make it a braggable session for her. She hasn't had anything to brag about in a long while, if you know what I mean."

My thirty minutes of mind debate was quickly settled when at my front door, with the world around us asleep, he murmured, "I'll call you," before making his way down the walkway to his car.

Although I was disappointed, the unmistakable sincerity in his voice compelled me to believe he wasn't like every other man, and that he would call.

Four

PAX DIDN'T CALL.

Not the following day, or the next, or even the following month.

Vanessa and Tom, who were inseparable the weeks following our dinner, by the end of the summer went their separate way. As was always the case, Vanessa broke up with Tom when he began getting too close, claiming he was clingy and needy. The breakup left her devastated, as they always did, at least until the next man came along. That, however, meant I couldn't find out about Pax.

I didn't dare call Pax, not because I didn't want to, but because actions like those were not in my DNA—or, more to the point, it wasn't the way I was raised. "Natalia, women do not call men." My mother's hectoring voice sounded off in my head each time my anxious hand reached for the telephone.

I thought of Pax often, at times with disappointment, but mostly with regret accompanied with tears. He resurrected feelings of loneliness I'd insulated myself from and had long ago compartmentalized in the recesses of my mind. He made it obvious that I had no one. No one to love or to love me back, no one to share my bed with, to talk to, or to think of when I listened to a beautiful piece of music. I suddenly ached for all those things. The pain of loneliness unbearable, I desperately tried to erase him from my mind. And in time I did.

In the months that followed, to distract from my dreary life, I busied myself with work and my schoolchildren. I volunteered to direct that year's Christmas play, which I knew would take up most of my spare time. And it did. It was a welcome distraction from my lonely existence.

On my free nights, I met Vanessa and the gang for dinner. Sensing the hole in my life that Pax had left, Vanessa began to make more time for me and showed up to our dinners alone. A nice gesture on her part, since she'd quickly found a replacement for Tom in John, who was shortly after replaced by Anthony, and in a matter of two weeks was replaced by... I'd lost track by then. Men gravitated to her like bees to their queen.

God, I envied her feminine magnetism, something I clearly lacked. Vanessa was fun, exciting, and adventurous. I was conservative, careful, and a pragmatist. She was the strapless dress with high slit skirts type, and I was the turtleneck with knee-length skirt kind of woman. And although I didn't think I was bad looking, I considered myself average to Vanessa's exotic good looks. She had the type of striking bronzed skin that most of us spend hours under the sun to capture if only to last for a few weeks. Her large almond-shaped eyes were the color of emeralds, a sprinkling of freckles on the tip of a dainty upturned nose and full lips were set on a delicate oval face. She had a dark, thick spill of waves that fell to smooth shoulders and a body that boasted nothing but sensuous curves.

Vanessa had been my best friend since grade five, when she'd come to my rescue after Stan, the class bully, had forced me to hand over my lunch money. At five feet eight inches, she had been the tallest kid in school. Towering over Stan, she'd looked down at him, arms crossed, foot impatiently tapping, and had demanded the return of my stolen money.

"Don't return the money, and my posse will come down on you with a vengeance. And believe me when I tell you that you don't want that, Stan," Vanessa had said. Not only had she got my money back with interest, but from that moment on Stan had become our protector.

Each time we reflected on the incident, we laughed until tears filled our eyes.

"There was never any posse. I just knew that what Stan made up in brawn, he lacked in the brain department. And as long as I was forceful enough, he'd believe anything I said. It's the genetic makeup of a bully." Vanessa laced her coffee with sugar and stirred.

"Lucky for me you did come to my rescue. Otherwise, we would have never ended up friends." I took the seat next to her after returning the coffee pot to the warming plate.

"Why not?"

"You were one scary bitch, and a shy, meek girl like me would have never dreamed of starting a conversation with you, let alone thought about becoming part of your inner circle. Can I have the sugar?"

She slid the bowl toward me. "Really, I scared you?" she said topping her fork with a piece of apple pie and an equal amount of vanilla ice cream. I felt the calories comfortably settling on my thighs just by watching her. The woman could eat anything she wanted and never gain a pound.

"You scared us all."

"Well, good," she said, sounding proud of the fact.

"Good? I say this with love, but you're still one scary bitch when you want to be." Not able to hold out any longer, I reached for the pie and saw her lips curl into a smile.

"I was wondering how long it would take for you to cave." She slid the vanilla ice cream toward me. "I hope I still am. A bitch, that is. It's taken me years to earn that badge and I wear it proudly."

"I'll put your mind at ease by telling you that you are. A super bitch, that is. But I love you just the same," I said. I considered her more of a sister than I did Caterina.

"What? I'm going for a run later today. It's why I took it up. Do you really think I love the sport? I run so I can indulge in sinfully delicious sweets and fattening carbs," she said when I rolled my eyes in disbelief as she set a second piece of apple pie on her plate and topped it with a generous dollop of ice cream. "Anyway, if you love me, then you must trust me."

Knowing exactly where the conversation was heading, I waved a hand in objection. "No, no, no, no, no."

"That's a record of five nos." She counted them off on her finger before shoveling more pie and ice cream into her mouth.

"You know blind dates never work out, especially when I'm involved."

"You have anything better going?"

She knew I didn't, and although I didn't answer right away, she also knew I'd eventually give in.

THE FIRST DATE VANESSA HAD SET me up on we'd double dated, but only because Lorenzo was Bart's—her current beau's—identical twin. I'd never met two men who were more different.

Bart was outgoing, intelligent, a chatterbox, and Lorenzo was none of those things. We went to dinner and a movie. I forget which film we saw or what we had for dinner. All I remembered was that at the end of the night, when Lorenzo reached in to kiss me good night, I rolled my car window up on him.

My second date was more memorable than my night with Lorenzo, but only because Robert corrected me when I mistakenly called him Rob.

"My name is Robert, not Rob or Bert. It's Robert," he was quick to point out. I was never into humorless, uptight twits. Rob, needless to say, never called again.

The dates that followed fared no better, whether because I was comparing them to Pax or because I didn't have what men wanted was up for debate. I started getting an inferiority complex. I began to doubt myself as a woman. I felt unattractive, uninteresting, unexciting, and so many other uns. I began to think of myself as too closed-minded, not adventurous or exciting enough. I began to think I was too demanding or maybe expected too much from a man and that I should settle.

Settling was what I did best.

Five

FALL QUICKLY TURNED to winter, and bare trees were clad in white, as were the roads, sidewalks, and rooftops. Christmas was a couple of weeks away, and it was then when the unexpected package landed on my doorstep. With curiosity, I eyed the small box wrapped in gold foil and topped with a red bow, and ventured to read the sender's name. My eyes rounded wide when I saw the name Pax Reed. It had been five months, one hundred and sixty-one days since I last saw or heard from the man I'd fallen in love with at first sight, and I wasn't sure whether to be indifferent or thrilled that he finally made contact. Indifference won out. The idea that after so many months he thought he could snake his way back into my life with a store-bought gesture made my chest tighten into that familiar ball of anger.

I tossed the unopened package—bow and all—into the garbage.

The package was still there the next day, and the following, and each time I walked past it thereafter. By the third day, curiosity got the better of me, and I fished it out of the garbage. Wiping off coffee grounds, a chicken bone, and wilted lettuce, from the wrapping, I set the box on the kitchen counter. I poured myself an indulgent glass of wine, sipped, and stared. I sipped and stared my way through two glasses before I mustered the courage to loosen the bow, tear the wrapping off and flip the lid open. Wordlessly, I found myself staring at the contents. There, nestled amongst the neatly crinkled red and green tissue paper, was a bottle of Destiny, my favourite perfume.

The simple gesture spoke volumes, and I felt the tears slipping from between closed lashes.

You see, it wasn't as simple as Pax walking up to the perfume counter at the local department store, asking for the bottle and handing over his credit card. It was much more complicated than that, since not once did my perfume preference come up for discussion during our one encounter months ago. Men didn't discuss such things. The thought that he had devoted so much effort to matching a scent he'd inscribed to memory made my heart bloom with love.

I ventured to open the enclosed note.

> *I know I don't deserve*
> *your forgiveness,*
> *but I'm asking for it.*
> *I would love to see you.*
> *Pax*

With my mother's advice not to call him screaming in my head, I reached for the telephone book, and called Pax to ask him out on our first official date.

PAX SUGGESTED WE MEET FOR DINNER at The Bistro. He wanted to start fresh and thought the restaurant where we'd first met was the ideal place.

With a cold, biting December wind, I made my way to The Bistro. The Beaches was ablaze in multicolored Christmas lights that hung from lampposts. Storefront windows were dressed in the spirit of the season with toy soldiers and Santa Clauses, and nativity scenes set atop white felt made out to look like snow. A blanket of freshly lain snow had caped the city, and I could hear the subtle crunch of it underfoot. It was a magical scene.

As our meeting time drew nearer, I felt excitement surge in me. I'd been looking so forward to this moment since Pax and I last spoke five days ago that I'd even succumbed to marking the days off on my calendar the way I used to as a child when a special occasion was forthcoming. And although it was only dinner, it felt like the promise of something exciting and new.

Not wanting to appear overly anxious, I walked into The Bistro fashionably late. It was fifteen minutes past our seven-p.m. meeting time. As calmly as I could make myself appear, I searched the crowded room for Pax.

I scanned the faces at the busy bar, where old friends caught up and new friends were coming together. A few of the regulars waved at me. Pax wasn't amongst them. I skimmed a glance over to the dining room, where a diverse crowd of patrons occupied almost every table. An elderly couple clinked glasses before they cut into their meal. A group of business suits, ties loosened, collar button undone, stiff drinks in hand, filled the long corner table. A family of four settled into the table next to them while at the opposite end of the room a group of young women collapsed into laughter when their friend's face contorted in a series of comical expressions as she recounted her story.

Pax wasn't anywhere to be seen.

None of them was Pax. I'd been stood up by him— again.

My teenage-like enthusiasm at the prospect of seeing him again quickly deflated like a child's smile at the sight of a present-less tree on Christmas day. Resentment and anger wove tightly at the pit of my stomach.

"You won't be staying, ma'am?" With the undertones of sisterly empathy in her voice, the hostess, a busty blonde in a tight-fitting black dress, asked.

I gave her the subtlest headshake, and, feeling the weight of countless piteous eyes on me, with my head bowed in embarrassment I made my way to the door. I wondered if I'd ever set foot in The Bistro again, where I'd spent a portion of my life celebrating birthdays, anniversaries, and engagements with friends. All those fond memories were now marred. The anger bubbled in me, not at Pax, but at myself for allowing it to happen. I should have never allowed him into my life. My heart was wounded, my self-esteem shattered, and I wasn't sure if they would ever heal.

With humiliation drowning me, I made my way to the front door. Just as I reached for the brass handle, the door flew open. A chilly air poured into the room and hit me, but all I could feel was the burn in my belly. Instinctively, I stepped aside to allow the person at the door entry. It was then the familiar voice came at me.

"Hi," he uttered in a breathless whisper.

My eyes drifted up to him. He was trying to catch his breath and his face was flush, I think more so from running than from the biting cold wind. I said nothing.

"I'm...I'm so sorry I'm late. My meeting at work ran late and I couldn't get to a telephone to call you. Then when I could, I didn't want to waste any time and thought it best to get into my car and rush over here. Then the traffic," he stopped for breath. "I'm sorry. I rushed here as fast as I could." His blue eyes tender in apology arrowed into my heart and weakened me.

My burgeoning resentment for him fading, I debated whether to swallow my pride or push on with rushing past him and out the door as I should have done. Part of me wanted to leave him standing there, feeling the burn of rejection just as I had felt six months earlier. Pax's eyes locked on mine, and although I knew I should hold on to my anger and lash out, the flash of heat in my eyes dissipated like steam in cold air. I was drowning in those lake-blue eyes, and seeing him there, standing before me, made everything right with the world again.

Weakness was clearly my strength.

"I understand," I said. "This is for you." Pax handed me the white rose he held.

How such a small gesture weakened my defenses is beyond comprehension, but it did, and I reached for it. "Thank you."

"Would you like to check your coats so I can show you to your table?" The hostess's voice cut into the awkward silence.

"Yes," Pax said and proceeded to help me out of my coat.

As the hostess led us through the restaurant, Pax rested a hand on my back, and my stomach did that little flip I'd felt on the night we kissed. I let the sensation wash over me, and hoped the feeling would last forever.

"You look stunning, by the way." Pax's voice warm and rich in my ear liquefied every bone in my body and I felt my knees turn to jelly.

I would never again doubt Vanessa. I don't know how long I'd spent searching through my closet for the right outfit when Vanessa sauntered into my bedroom, a mischievous grin on her face and a ridiculously short, low V-neck dress in her hands. When my jaw dropped to the ground she was quick to point out, "Oh, Natalia, it's Christmas for God sakes and this fiery red color is perfect." The dress, which hugged more tightly than I felt comfortable with, went against my conservative nature and I quickly dismissed it. I was glad now she pushed hard enough for me to reconsider the glittery number she guaranteed would mesmerize him into a trance, as it did then.

"Thank you," was all I said and looked away when I decided of not letting on how I thought he look like the most handsome man in the room in the black, double-breasted suit against the taupe shirt. Some things, I thought, were best left unsaid.

We ordered drinks and dinner, and easily fell into the rhythm we'd shared that first night. I wanted to ask him why he'd waited as long as he had to call me, but thought better of it, deciding it wasn't the best lead-in to the evening. He was here now, and that was all that mattered to me. We spent hours talking. Our conversation, drifting easily from one subject to another, was anything but mundane. This time around we spoke more intimately, telling one another about our dreams, our wants, our likes and dislikes.

After the server set dessert before us, Pax's eyes drifted up to me.

"I'm sorry I didn't reach out to you until now."

I stared at him over the rim of my wine glass. Although the night had already made up for my wounded pride, I wanted an explanation. I deserved one, damn it.

"I think I mentioned that I'd moved back home to care for my ailing mother." Pax's expression turned contemplative, and I fell into the silence that followed with him. He let the air out of his lungs and on a long sigh said, "She lost her battle." His voice broke. "Lung cancer. She passed away a few weeks after we met. And then everything snowballed…" His thoughts trailed to what I presumed were memories of her.

Something inside my belly clenched when pained eyes looked in my direction, and instinctively, I reached for his hand and let it linger "Oh, Pax…I'm so sorry."

He wrapped his hand tightly around mine. It was large, warm, manly, and as solemn as the moment was, I was suddenly conscious of how long it had been since I'd felt the touch of a man.

Pax remained quiet for a long while. During his introspective pause, he never once let go of my hand, I think partly because it offered a comfort he needed then and partly because he needed to touch life.

With a glint of tears in his eyes, Pax went on. "It wasn't as if her death was unexpected, but it was still difficult. She was the only family I had left." The pain in his voice ran deep.

The realization of what he'd gone through doused me with a splash of reality, and it made my heart ache. Guilt smothered me. The idea that I'd spent all those months wallowing in self-pity when he was going through such a difficult ordeal made me feel stupid, selfish, and sick to my stomach.

Thinking better than to offer the sympathetic clichés reserved for such moments, I let him talk. And he did. Pax's voice was surprisingly steady, but I could hear the sorrow in his tone as he told me all about his mother: her illness, the pain, the suffering she'd endured at the hands of the cancer that had ravaged her body slowly and painfully.

Through it all, I could see the love for his mother in his eyes as the memories played in his mind. It was as if all those things he'd wanted to say came to the surface, and I was pleased he'd turned to me.

"She sounds like she was a bright spirit. Someone I would like to have known."

"She would have liked you, Natalia." The words tapered off to a faint smile.

I said the first thing that came to mind then. "You're a good son, Pax, and I'm sure she was proud of you."

"Thank you for saying so." There was a beat of silence. "It's the reason I didn't call you."

The explanation I'd wanted all these months now seemed frivolous and I said, "You don't have to explain."

"I do. You deserve an explanation. It was just me, and between taking care of her, work, and then having to make funeral arrangements and taking care of her affairs afterwards, it was just…"

The look of pain in his eyes arrowed into my heart and at that moment I saw the man before me with perfect clarity. Quite simply, I'd fallen in love with him. "Pax, I'm sorry I wasn't…" a better person, "I'm sorry you had to go through this on your own."

Eyes on me, he squeezed my hand.

My stomach knotted a little tighter, and my eyes drifted away from him. He needed a friend and all I knew to do was to think of myself. "I should have made an effort to…"

"Don't torture yourself, Natalia. You didn't know." He leaned forward, tucked a strand of my hair behind my ear. "I'm happy you're here now."

"Me too." I wanted to reach for his hand and press it to my cheek.

"Are you going to share that piece of cake?" Pax asked with a wide smile.

"If I must."

We split the piece of double fudge cake, eating our way in from opposite sides until only a sliver was left, which he motioned me to claim.

"Did I get the perfume right? Destiny, I think it was," he said setting his credit card down in the billfold, sliding it to the edge of the table.

My throat tightened at the thought of how the incredible gesture he'd made for me during such a difficult time in his life. "You did."

"I'm glad." He held out his hand, and with the pang of regret that the most memorable night of my life was coming to an end, I took it.

WHEN WE STEPPED OUT OF THE restaurant, a white moon cast a silver glow over the city, and snowflakes danced in the wind that carried in it a sharp taste of winter. The scene was serene, one of storybook beauty and I was thrilled to be sharing it with Pax.

"I'll walk you to your car," he said and when he laced his fingers with mine, he sent a wave of heat through my entire body.

"All right," I said thrilled to have a few more minutes with him.

Together, in a comfortable silence we made the one-block walk to the nearly empty parking lot. At my car, despite the steady fall of snow, we stood for a long silent moment, our eyes fixed on one another as if nothing else existed, mattered.

Pax ran a gentle hand over my shoulders, dusting the snow away, then ran his hands up and down my arms for warmth. I pressed closer, absorbing the scents that were part of him, man and musky. It was intoxicating. When he moved closer, I leaned into him. Cupping a hand under my chin, he brought my face up to meet his, the heat from his breath billowing in the air as he moved closer. When his mouth met mine, he kissed me tenderly, lovingly. His mouth was hot, and his lips were moist. My breath caught when I felt the erotic slide of his tongue parting my lips. Savoring the taste of wine on it, enjoying the sensation of his lips, of his breath, a flood of liquid heat raced through my veins and made my skin tingle.

We kissed for a long time, oblivious to the falling snow or the cold air biting at our heels. I didn't want the moment to end. From the hunger in his kiss, I sensed Pax didn't either.

We kissed until we were both breathless.

Eventually, Pax pulled back, searching my face. Blue eyes swelling with emotion met mine. "I missed you. I'm not used to missing anyone. No other woman has made me feel the way you do, but my emotions may be too unpredictable right now."

I felt something collapse inside me.

"I don't want to hurt you, Natalia."

Blinking the tears burning in my eyes away, I said nothing.

He held me then. Feeling the warmth of his body against my own made me realize how much I needed him, and I braced myself for the worst.

"I know it's crazy. I mean, we've only just met, but during the past few months, I couldn't stop thinking of you. Thoughts of you filled me day and night. You were in my every thought, my dreams. I haven't been able to put you out of my mind. It's what kept me going." He cupped my chin and lifted my face up to his. "Does all this sound irrational to you?"

I swallowed, feeling the dryness in my throat as my own feelings stirred in me. Unable to trust my voice, I gave a subtle headshake.

"My head is not screwed on right, right now, and the last thing I want to do is hurt you. But..." He paused as if trying to organize his thoughts. I felt his thumb idly tracing the contours of my hand as he considered his next words. Then turning his gaze to me he said, "I think I'm falling in love with you. But I don't want..."

The tears backing up in my throat, I raised a finger to his lips. "I think I'm falling in love with you, Pax." I knew then I wanted to spend the rest of my life with this man.

AGAINST MY MOTHER'S WISHES, PAX AND I were married three months later in an intimate church ceremony. I wore a white Christian Dior strapless trumpet gown, with a jade drop necklace that Pax said brought out the color in my eyes. He wore a chocolate colored, double-breasted suit against an indigo silk shirt and a matching tie that brought out the blueness in his. Before fifty family members and friends, and with Vanessa as my maid of honor and Tom as the best man, Pax and I pledged our love to one another.

And so began our journey as Mr. and Mrs. Reed.

It was a journey that would test our marriage, bring endless heartache, and prove that only when bonds are tested do we understand their strengths.

Six

OUR HONEYMOON WAS exciting and exotic, everything I'd dreamed of. We visited thirteen European countries in thirty days. It was a lifelong dream of mine, and one I was thrilled to share it with Pax.

The romantic city of Venice was our first stop and where a gondolier serenaded us as we glided through the narrow backstreet canals. Later that day, with curtains billowing in the light breeze flowing through the opened window of our hotel room, as the sun painting the sky crimson and gold over the still waters of the *Golfo Di Venezia*, we made love for the first time as husband and wife.

His mouth took mine with passion and desire, and his hands explored the depths of my body with such a light, but expert, touch that left me begging for more, wanting it to never end. And when we joined, it was fulfilling, and beautiful, and I'd never felt more loved. Crying in his arms, I thanked him for being in my life.

Pax and I went on to visit London, Paris, Switzerland, Frankfurt, and Vienna. Our days were spent touring historic landmarks, walking down cobbled roads and dining at wonderful restaurants. Nights were spent in bed, drinking fantastic wines, and making love. Every city became a notable memory. In Naples, we skipped over to the island of Capri to take in the magical, dream-like blue waters of the *Grotta Azzurra*. It was everything I'd read about, and the experience felt momentous because I was sharing it with Pax.

We made our way up the coastline of the spectacular French Riviera, where the Alps come down within reach of the Mediterranean water's edge. We visited Cannes, where once a year directors and actors flocked to for the international film festival. We sipped on cappuccino at an outside café where Cary Grant, Sophia Loren, and Elizabeth Taylor frequented during their stay. In exotic Monaco, we walked up the steps of the Monte Carlo casino, which until then I'd only seen in a James Bond movie. Pax and I posed for pictures in character. In Paris, as the bateaux mouche crossed at the base of the Eiffel tower, amidst hundreds of tourists, Pax kissed me as he'd dreamed of doing with his wife and I did so because it made him happy.

I'd never been happier. It had all been perfect, completely and wonderfully perfect. We returned home tired, but exhilarated to begin creating our new life together.

We settled into Pax's childhood home, a two-story, red brick house, with the glass enclosed solarium, overlooking the grove of hundred-year-old pines, evergreens, and maple. It wasn't a large home, but it was ideal for our family to be. Like me, Pax wanted to have children—lots of them.

When Monday rolled around, Pax returned to Roth & Associates, and I went back to St. Mary's Elementary where my twenty children welcomed me with a handmade card, signed by everyone in an array of colorful crayons. I read the card aloud, as the children watched on beaming with pride at their handiwork.

"We all made it for you, Mrs. Rossi." Wyatt's cherubic face brimmed with a smile.

The children giggled, and together corrected Wyatt. "It's Mrs. Reed, Wyatt."

Wyatt's innocence puckered in apology. "I'm sorry...ah, Mrs. Reed. And, oh yeah, I'm supposed to say welcome home."

Mrs. Reed was home.

PAX AND I SETTLED INTO OUR new routine and fell into harmony with one another.

We were perfect together. I loved waking up next to Pax, and breathing in the smell of him, at first light. I looked forward to falling asleep in his arms at night, and I loved the feel of his body pressed against mine before he dozed off to sleep.

I couldn't wait to get home to him to have our after-work talks and sharing every aspect of my day with him as he intently listened and hung on my every word. And each night, over dinner and a glass of wine, he'd tell me about his day or we'd talk about anything and everything, regardless how important or insignificant.

Once talked out, Pax cleared the table and I washed the dishes. Afterwards I'd putter around the house or in the garden, putting my touch on our home, before settling into the sitting room in the solarium to correct papers or prepare the next day's lesson. Pax headed off to his office to catch up on paperwork, or the mounds of reading his job demanded.

At the end of the day, Pax and I made our way up the stairs to our bedroom. With moonlight streaming through the window, fingers unbuttoned shirts and unclasped jeans, and flooded with desire we made love, discovering one another the way newlyweds do, before falling asleep in each other's arms into dreams.

It was the idyllic life that no one—least of all me—thought it would ever end up making me question the foundations of my marriage.

Seven

Vanessa

NATALIA WENT LIMP. "Vanessa's in ICU because she had a seizure? But she's never been afflicted with seizures before."

Tom wavered, and Natalia sensed there was more that needed to be told.

"What is it, Tom?" Anxiously, Natalia waited for him to say something.

"Where's Pax?"

"He's parking the car. He should be here soon."

Tom walked to the window. A curtain of white cascaded out of a blackened sky to coat everything in its path. Tom saw none of it. He simply stood there motionless, his eyes focused on some distant point.

"Tom?" Natalia broke the threads of his thoughts, and he turned back to face Natalia.

"Let's wait for Pax."

The silence that fell between them was smothering.

"I'm sorry I took so long." Pax and Tom's hands met briefly. "Plows are out and I had to wait for a spot. Any word on Vanesa?"

Natalia shook her head. "Pax is here now, Tom. What was it that you couldn't tell me until he got here?"

It took Tom a moment to respond. "Vanessa's parents are…are dead. They…died on impact."

Shock struck hard and as Tom's words rang in Natalia's ears, her stomach began to turn. There were so many questions she needed to ask, but the words got stuck in a sandpaper dry throat. Natalia remained silent for a long while as she processed the words, the shock, the surreal moment.

"Jesus." Pax made a sound between a sigh and gasp. "You said on impact. What does that mean, Tom?"

"A fourteen-wheeler hauling sewer pipes hit an icy patch of road. The truck driver tried to make a quick correction, but the roads were too slick. He swerved to avoid hitting the van in front of him and ended up sideswiping Vanessa's car, sending it straight into the concrete wall of the Don Mills Bridge. Her parents were in the front and back seats of the right side of the car. The side that made contact with the wall. They…" Tom grew quiet for a moment, then, in almost a whisper, said, "They were gone the moment the car hit the wall."

"Oh my God!" Natalia's voice trembled when she spit out the words.

Tom looked down at his hands as if entranced by them. "Vanessa miraculously survived with minor bruises, and was conscious and lucid when they brought her in. I'd been talking to her for well over an hour, when the first seizure hit and…I couldn't do anything for her." There was guilt and shock in his eyes.

Bolting to her feet, Natalia crossed to where Tom stood and wrapped her arms around him. "I'm sorry, Tom. You did what you could, and I'm sure she was glad it was you by her side. I know she couldn't have asked for a better friend to be with her. I need to see her. I need to see her now."

"They're taking care of her. It's what she needs right now." Pax's words stopped Natalia at the doorway. "Best to let the doctor and nurses tend to her right now. They know we're here. They'll come get us when they're ready." Taking Natalia's hand, Pax walked her back to the line of chairs.

"Her mother and father were the only family she had." Natalia looked into Pax's eyes then, turned to Tom. "Does she know they're…gone?"

Tom shook his head. "I asked the medical team not to mention anything to her. I led her to believe they were receiving medical attention on another floor. Getting an EKG, and x-rays to check for broken bones. I wanted to wait until the…right time, until she was able to take the shock."

Natalia fell into the silence Tom left until the thought hit her. "If you were with them, why aren't you hurt? Why were you even with them, Tom?"

"It was a…business dinner. I was getting her parents to sign off on some legal documents Vanessa had me draught up. The weather was getting worse and Vanessa asked them to take a taxi home, but they refused to leave their car at my place so she decided to drive them home, and I followed behind to drive her back to my place to pick up her car. I was a few cars behind, following Vanessa. I…saw the entire thing happen." Tom's voice became strangled.

Pure shock had Pax and Natalia staring at Tom. Natalia's mind flashing to that moment in time, she pictured the terrified look on Vanessa and her parents' faces when she lost control of the car. Natalia imagined the look of despair on Vanessa's face when, for an instant, the world must have seemed to move in slow motion before she realized there was no turning back.

Natalia couldn't begin to imagine the horror coursing through Tom as he watched the car careen out of control. She wondered what Vanessa's parents last thoughts were when they sensed they were going to die. Natalia heard their screams in her head, and her stomach knotted so tight it felt as if someone had driven a hard fist right into the center of it.

She reached for Tom's hand. "I'm so sorry."

"I followed the ambulance to the hospital. I wasn't even sure what to expect of Vanessa's condition. I wasn't sure if she was alive or..." His voice trailed off, sounding far away.

Natalia went numb at the realization that Tom had stopped short at the word dead. Suddenly, she felt fragile. She closed her eyes, hoping to wake up from the nightmare that seemed to be going on forever, but when she opened them, she was still in the small, dreary room with the brash, cold fluorescent lights. That redolent hospital smell that induced instant dread was now attached to her clothes, to every part of her.

"I need to see her now. I need to know how she is. I need to make sure she's alive." Tired, much too tired to do anything else, Natalia buried her face in her hands and let the tears flow.

Eight

TIME, AS IT tends to do, slipped away from us, and before Pax and I knew it, we were celebrating our first anniversary.

"Happy anniversary, Mrs. Reed," the children sang out when I walked into the classroom that morning. Each held a long stem, white rose.

"Thank you, children, this is lovely, but how could you possibly have known?" The question set the children into giggles.

"Ith a thecret Mithess Reed." Janice, my toothless beauty, lisped before she tapped Matthew on the shoulder. "Go ahead."

"This is for you, Mrs. Reed." Matthew handed me his rose.

"You forgot to give her the card," Tania whispered over Matthew's shoulder.

"Oh yeah," Matthew dug into his jeans pocket and handed me the crumpled envelope along with a bubble gum wrapper, complete with a wad of gum, two bottle caps, an eraser, and a plastic snake. "You're supposed to read it, Mrs. Reed. The note that is."

And I did so.

In a world where dreams are few
You made mine come true when I found
you
My life is complete
Now that you're in it
You will always be in my heart
You will always be the only woman I'll
ever want.
Pax

"She muth really like what Mither Reed wrote in the card. She's thmiling tho much," Janice said, and the children nodded in agreement.

"What does your card say, Mrs. Reed?" Matthew asked with the curious gaze of a seven-year-old.

As I was about to answer, Matthew and the children, looking past me to the doorway, broke out in giggles. I turned to see Pax with a four-foot-tall teddy bear. With arms wrapped around Teddy, he ambled toward me and planted a kiss on my cheek—to the oohs and aahs of giggling children.

"Happy anniversary." His lips curled into the smile I'd fallen in love with.

"Happy anniversary and thank you, this is all very lovely."

"I'm glad you like it."

"Mither Reed, we did what you athked right?" Janice said looking up to Pax with innocent doe eyes.

"You did, Janice. Thank you so much for helping me put this together for Mrs. Reed. You did a fantastic job. And as per our agreement, here's your payment. Now make sure to share it with everyone." Pax handed a wide-eyed Janice the large bag of candies.

"Well, that's not going to get me in trouble with the parents."

"What? These children were really tough on me. They wore me down to a giant bag of candy in return for their silence to put this on. They're the toughest negotiators I've faced yet. And that Janice, I have to tell you, that even with that delightful lisp of hers, she can reduce a grown man to groveling on his knees," Pax said with an unwavering expression that made me break down in laughter.

When I finally managed to stop laughing, I turned to the children who were about to dig into the candy bag. "You can all have one piece now. We'll split the rest of the candy together during math hour and you'll tuck it into your lunch boxes to show your parents when you get home tonight." I waited for the grunts to die down before giving Janice the go ahead to open the giant bag again.

"I get the flowers, but what's he for?" I gestured toward the giant bear, which the children now had taken control over.

"It's for our baby."

"But how did you know?"

His expression contorted into one of confusion. "Know what?"

"That I'm pregnant."

The stunned look on his face said it all and for a long while, Pax remained silent processing what I'd said. "You're…"

"Pregnant. I'm pregnant." My words tumbled out in excitement when I finished his thought. "If you didn't know then…" I pointed over at Teddy, who Nora and Jack were attempting to hoist into the chair behind my desk, as the children called out instructions.

"He was supposed to be an incentive, but never mind him now. Are you really..." A stunned Pax rested his hand on my tummy, over the child that was growing inside of me. "Pregnant?"

"I am. This is your baby, our baby," I said, lowering my hand over his.

Pax linked fingers with mine. "Sweets, this is the best anniversary gift you could give me."

THAT NIGHT WITH THE SOUND OF crackling logs in the fireplace drifting in the stillness of our home, Pax and I celebrated our news and our first anniversary. Sharing a pizza on the white shag carpet, we spoke about our baby, and the momentous changes coming our way. Pax was as excited as I was about the pregnancy, and although I never expected otherwise, the reality of the moment made it that much more wonderful.

"Why didn't you tell me you were pregnant sooner?" Pax set two pizza slices on my plate and poured apple juice into my glass.

"I wanted to be sure before I said anything. I didn't want to...disappoint you. I wanted to wait until I got the results from the doctor to tell you. I only found out yesterday, and I thought I'd surprise you on our anniversary." The flickering flames from the fireplace danced in surprised blue eyes.

He reached for my hand raised it to his lips. "Sweets, you can never disappoint me. Why would you even think that?"

"I know how much you want to have children and I wanted to be sure before saying anything and raising your hopes." With no family except me to call his own, I desperately wanted to make that wish a reality for him, for the two of us. "I'm sorry I didn't tell you as soon as I found out."

"I want to share in everything with you. The great, the doubts, the fears." Pax said it so sweetly that I felt closer to him than ever.

"I have a doctor's appointment on Monday at ten." A warmth, redolent with the faint scent of pine struck me.

"Would you like me to go with you?" Pax poured wine into his glass.

"If you'd like to, but it's not necessary. On this visit, she's going talk to me about what to expect and run some blood tests and a pee test."

"I'm going with you. It sounds like you'll need some serious ass back-up there. You know how difficult it is for women to aim into that small cylindrical cup," he said with a smirk reaching for his second slice of pizza.

"I can see how that's a problem. This is going to be so great, Pax. There's nothing more in the world I want than to have a baby that's ours."

His glass of wine abruptly paused mid-air. "I'm going to be a daddy." The dazed, stunned look came with shock.

"Yes, you are, and you're going to be a great one." I rested my hand on the floating one and brought glass and hand to rest on the coffee table. The doubtful expression in the usual confident face surprised me.

"You think so? It's a huge responsibility." His mind deep in thought, his fingers absently ran up and down the stem of his wine glass. "Am I up to it? I mean, this is a helpless human being I'll be responsible for…for the rest of their life." Tilting back his glass, he drained his wine.

"You're up to it. And besides, I'm going to be right there with you." I squeezed his hand in reassurance, but all I got was a weary look. "You're going to be a great father."

Sapphire blue eyes flickered up to mine, and I could see anxiety brimming in them. "I don't know anything about being a father. I'm so glad you're not able to drink tonight. I'm going to need this entire bottle," he said topping his glass of wine to the rim.

"No one knows anything about being a parent. At least that's what my children's mothers tell me." My words did nothing to assuage his rattled nerves, and he guzzled half his wine. "All I know is that you're a wonderful, loving, caring husband, the sweetest man I know, and its traits like those that will make you a great father." My comment put a smile on his face, and I saw him breathe a sigh of relief.

Pizza eaten, I cleared the coffee table of dishes, glasses, the three-quarter empty wine bottle and pizza box while Pax added a couple of logs to the fireplace.

The flames spreading again, he sat next to me on the carpet and I snuggled up against him, resting my head on his shoulder.

"Thank you."

I tilted my gaze up to him. "For what?"

"For marrying me. Without you, I'm nothing. This has been the best year of my life." His hand traveled down to my belly and let it rest there. "And now you having our baby is wonderful and amazing." He fell silent for a moment. "I love you more than the night is dark and the day is bright, Mrs. Reed."

There was love there, the kind that lasted lifetimes. I'd never felt more loved than I did then, and I knew I could live to be one hundred and never love anyone as I did him.

I kissed him this time, wanting to feel his warm lips on mine. "I've never been happier than I am right now. I feel like a bird soaring high in the sky, able to reach heights I never could before. And you made that happen."

"I hope she looks like you." The way he said it made my throat close a little.

I leaned back, trying to catch a glimpse of his face. "She? You don't want a boy?"

"I want a little girl just like her mother." His voice, tender and loving, made my world seem dreamlike.

With a lump forming in my throat, I brought my hand to his face and touched his cheek. It felt so right to be with him, to be linked with him through the life growing in me. Leaning in, I kissed him and I felt his love flow through me, in me.

His arms chained around me, he pressed his body to mine. The heat from our bodies flowing between us, I slid my hand beneath his shirt, over his firm chest. His body trembled with the same anticipation that mine did.

The fire flickering in the fireplace made shadows stretch and dance around us. Pax brought our joined hands to his lips, brushed my knuckles. Drawing me close, he skimmed his mouth over mine. It was a teasing, whisper of a kiss, a tender glide of lips against lips to whet my appetite. He smelled of man, desire, and want. It made me crave for more, demand more. When I did, he poured himself into the kiss. His mouth, hot and moist, crushed down on mine. It was all demand and when his tongue joined mine in a rhythmic dance, I could taste the hint of wine on it. His kiss deepening, I heard the throaty moans escape from both of us as the ache and urge for one another took control.

Blue eyes bursting with want and need stayed on me as he unzipped my dress and slid it off my shoulders. His breath quickening, his hands began to roam, seeking the depths of my body. Claiming it as his own, he sent frantic pulses of heat through my veins, under my skin, clouding my brain.

Resting my hands on his chest, I skated fingers down his shirt, slowly unbuttoning it. I had done this so many times before, and still the anticipation of our naked bodies coming together made me giddy and I began to tremble with the same anticipation I had felt the first time we came together.

I felt the rise and fall as his breaths quickening at my touch. Conscious of the way his body was responding, my fingers drifted over his chest through the thick, dark hair. I took my hands down the length of his stomach to the snap on his jeans.

The sound of crackling logs and our ragged breaths filled the silence of the room. Pax's mouth greedily clung to mine. "I want you so much. I need you so much."

"I've always only wanted you, Pax. Touch me, take me, love me, make me yours."

Pax's hands and mouth explored every inch of my body. He did things to me that made me cry out in the tender sounds of satisfaction that a woman shares with the man she loves. And with my mouth and hands I did the same for him. I filled him with the same pleasure he'd given me.

Whispering the words I loved to hear, he slipped inside me, slowly, lovingly, savoring the moment. Joined as one, our lovemaking went far beyond two bodies coming together in physical union. There was a spirituality and a passion I hadn't felt before. Pax was a great lover, gentle and caring, but tonight he was earthy and powerful, gentle yet animalistic. Our bodies alive, we catapulted with intensity and crested with unreserved abandonment, our cries filling the darkness.

We made love again an hour later, and when we joined as one then, my body reveled in the sensations only he could stir in me. Pulsing, throbbing for as long as humanly possible, he made the moment last forever before our bodies jointly shuddered and jerked from the last ferocious surge.

Slaked and content, wrapped in Pax's arms, we lay awake staring out the large window up to a round moon and the thousand stars twinkling in a black-blue sky.

"There goes a shooting star. Make a wish," I murmured when out the window I saw the streaking body of light flash across the sky.

Slumberous eyes looked at me. "I have everything I want," he said, pressing his lips over mine.

HIS NAKED BODY WAS STILL SPOONING mine when he fell asleep, and I thought back to that first night we'd made love, and how safe and loved I'd felt in his arms. I'd never forget how perfect and right he'd made it feel, and when he'd told me that we were meant to be together for all eternity, I'd believed him.

Now more than ever I believed we would be.

I thought of our baby, and my heart overflowed with emotion. It would now be three of us on this journey through life. The love I felt at that moment for Pax and my unborn child transcended anything I'd felt before. I knew then that nothing, no matter how momentous, would mean as much as the child inside me.

I thought about how much I was looking forward to the journey that would take us through our lifetime together. The blinding, searing joy at the thought of holding our baby in my arms for the first time made my throat constrict. I pictured her taking her first steps, saying her first word, which I'd ensure would be "Dada." I let the indescribable happiness wash over me as I pictured her graduating and going off to college. I imagined watching her walk down the aisle arm in arm with Pax to start a life of her own.

Pax stirred for a moment, and the image of him with our child in his arms flashed in my mind. And even with all his reservations about fatherhood, I knew he was going to be as perfect a father to our child as he could be, just as I was going to be as perfect a mother as I could be.

Lost in thought, I drifted into a baby-filled sleep.

Nine

THE MOMENT I opened my front door, sun poured in and bounced off the sweep of glossy white tiles of the foyer. A gentle breeze fragrant with spring and the scent of freshly cut grass drifted in the air. It was the kind of day that begged for children to be outdoors, for walkers to bask under its brightness, and sun worshippers to soak it in.

"Hi." Vanessa's sweaty face flashed a smile.

"Did you jog the ten miles from your home here?"

"I wasn't planning to, but once I started I couldn't stop." She tugged at the soaked T-shirt clinging to her body in an attempt to fan herself.

"I'm assuming you're thirsty."

"And hungry," she said in between breaths. "I hope that fresh apple pie smell is coming from your kitchen."

"It is, but it still needs another twenty minutes in the oven, and I need that time to finish marking the last handful of spelling tests. Why don't you take a shower? It should be ready by the time you come down. You know the way to the guest room, and where to find your spare clothes." She followed me into the house.

"You know we need coffee to go with that pie," she called out from the top of the stairs.

Looking up to her I said, "Of course, your Ladyship. I'll set it to brew right away."

Vanessa was as predictable as she was unpredictable. Although I never knew when to expect her visits, I knew they would happen after each breakup. It was all part of her dating M.O.: date a man for weeks, break up with him when he became too attached, reach out to me to vent. It was how it went down each time. And each time I'd be there with pie and ice cream, and a listening ear, because I was the only person Vanessa ever turned to in her moment of grief. I was the only person Vanessa confided her darkest secrets.

It went without saying that I understood why she delighted in her carefree life, why she jumped from man to man, never wanting anything more than a casual, sexual relationship from them. Unlike most who derided her carefree lifestyle, I understood that it was all an act on Vanessa's part. That her actions were simply an emotional shield she put around herself to guard from ever being hurt again. I knew that deep down what she really wanted was to fall in love, and settle into a meaningful and stable relationship, but that it was the demons in her past, wouldn't allow her to.

Although I didn't agree with her lifestyle, and I was certain she knew as much, I was her best friend, and best friends support one another through thick and thin. It was the pact we'd made to one another as children.

"You promise to always be there for me."

I nodded. "I promise."

Vanessa pressed her lips into a thin line and bobbed her head once. "Me too." She pressed the palm of her hand to mine and wrapped a pink ribbon around them. I pulled on

*one end and she on the other to seal the ribbon in place.
"You vow to do anything, anything for one another if it
meant the happiness of the other."*

*Me, the more timid of the two said, "What does anything
mean?"*

*"Would you lie to your mother or mine if it meant
protecting me?"*

*"I don't know if I can do that. My mom says she has this
hair at the back of her neck that tells her when I'm lying."*

*"Yeah, my mom says that too. Okay, how about, would
you lie to our teachers and Mrs. Pinkerton, our principal?"
she said still biting down on the pink ribbon.*

*I nodded at that. "Sure, I can. Just don't go getting into
as much trouble as you usually do?"*

*"Okay, I'll try. Repeat after me. I vow to you that I will
do anything, anything for one another if it means the
happiness and welfare of the other."*

Anything did take a different meaning through the
different stages of our life, but the pact remained as strong
in our adult life.

"How are baby and mommy?" Vanessa asked when she
joined me in the kitchen. Dressed in a fresh pair of jeans,
her feet were bare and the tips of her wet hair clung to the
neck of her white T-shirt.

My hand instinctively lowered to my tummy. "As
perfect as can be expected."

"Shouldn't you be off your feet or something?" She
bundled her wet hair into a smooth ponytail.

"I'm only on my eighth week. At this stage, exercise is
actually good for me. "Why don't you pour us each a cup of
coffee? I hope you don't mind decaf." With gloved hands, I
reached into the oven.

"Decaf's fine," she said, inhaling the fresh aroma the apple pie left in the air. "That smells glorious. I'm glad one of us learned to cook."

"Are you sure you want pie? I can make you something healthier. I'd hate for you to waste that run."

"Not only do I want pie, but I'm thinking it needs to be topped with a ginormous scoop of vanilla ice cream." Vanessa winked and turned to fill the second mug with coffee.

I cut a generous slice of pie and topped it with the requested dollop of vanilla ice cream. "Here you go."

"Is Pax home?" she mumbled between bites.

"No, he's at work, catching up on paperwork." I plated a piece half the size of Vanessa's, and topped it with less ice cream than I would have liked. Although I was eating for two, and certain the baby would love the taste of ice cream, unlike Vanessa, my body processed calories in an extraordinarily unfair manner.

"On a Sunday? That's dedication. It's no wonder they're considering fast-tracking him for partnership."

From my shocked expression, she could only deduce that was news to me.

"Me and my big mouth. Now Pax is really going to regret helping me get the paralegal job in his department. I just started working there and I'm already gossiping with you about work and I love that job, the people…"

I cut off her ramblings. "Never mind that. What's this about Pax being considered for partnership?"

Vanessa hesitated for a moment. "Oh, I've already blabbed it, so I may as well tell you what I know. But you can't tell anyone where you got it from. Promise me, Natalia."

Locking my lips with the make-believe key, I tossed it away as we'd done since we were children. "I promise to lock it in the vault."

She savored the bite of pie she'd forked into her mouth. "All right then, since you swore. Pax is on the short list to make partner. Apparently, bringing in the Stanton & Rossi account, along with all that other Stanton business elevates him to a top ten producer. You know in revenue and billable hours, and all that good stuff."

"Are you sure about this? When was it announced? Pax shouldn't be under consideration for some time yet."

"Well, it sort of hasn't been announced yet." Vanessa waved her coffee cup in the air.

"If it hasn't been announced, then how do you know?" I gave Vanessa a probing look, wondering where, as a paralegal, she'd come across such classified information.

"Ummm..." She started and did that contemplative eye roll I'd seen so many times when she fished in her brain through the hundreds of made up excuses she used to dissuade the men she had no interest in to move along.

"The truth, Vanessa. Was it Tom who told you this?"

Vanessa closed her hands around her coffee cup. "Tom and I right now are, let's just say, keeping our distance."

"You mean you're keeping your distance." That poor man, I thought. I'd never understand why he put up with so much from her. If only she could see how deeply in love, he was with her.

"Something like that. The man is just too clingy, and..."

I held up a hand. "Let's save that for our next topic of conversation. Right now, I want to know about the partnership."

"Well, I went out for drinks with one of the senior partners, and one thing led to another and…well, you know it became…pillow talk."

"So, this is reliable information?"

She raised a perfectly shaped brow. "Oh, believe me, honey. My pillow talker is as high up in the firm as they come. You can't tell Pax that I told you all this, Natalia. Neither Bobby nor Pax would be pleased with me. Not to mention Tom. Although we're broken up, I do like to keep him as back up."

"I'm not going to say anything, but…wait, what? Are you sleeping with Bobby Roth, the founder?"

"Junior, not senior, for God's sake. Senior is eighty." She gave a look of disgust. "How could you even think that?"

"Whether junior or senior, they're both married, Vanessa. And it's worse if it's Bobby Jr. He has a family, a wife and three young children." The sharpness of my tone took her aback. For the first time in our friendship, there was temper in my voice, and although I regretted it, I felt it justified.

Her lashes lowered, she set her focus on the dark liquid in her cup. "I know, but it's not as if he doesn't sleep around."

"That's not the point, Vanessa. Is it? Is this what you're doing now, sleeping with married men? I guess it's not enough that you've slept with practically half of the single men in town." It slipped out before I could catch myself and I slid into the awkward silence that now hung in the room.

The judgmental tone I promised never to use with her flowed from me without reservation, but it was one thing to parade single men in and out of your life, men who were accountable to no one but themselves. It was an entirely different matter to set out to destroy a home, a family. Besides, this was Pax's place of work. She was there because of him, and I thought she'd crossed the line of proper decorum. This wasn't easily going to be dismissed by my loyalty or her marred past.

"It just happened, and I didn't let it go beyond a few weeks." Her voice cut the thickening silence like honed Damascus steel.

Knowing my silence would unnerve her, I said nothing.

She bit down on her lower lip like a chastised little girl. "Honest. I put a stop to it right away."

Needing to distance myself before I hurled more words I would later regret, I rose from the table and busied myself with clearing the counter. I returned the pie-making ingredients I'd used earlier to the pantry and the refrigerator. The counter clean, I made my way to the sink and began to run a soapy sponge over the stack of dishes.

For a long while neither one of us spoke. The clanking of dishes as I washed and set them on the dishrack was the only sound filling the kitchen.

I understood Vanessa, knew that although Bobby had probably been the one to seduce her, I also knew she wouldn't have jumped into bed with him unless she wanted to. Vanessa didn't get used, she used. Contrary to what most believed, she discarded the men in her life not the other way around. And I understood that it was because of that sonofabitch Jameson that she did what she did. I understood that her actions stemmed from Jameson helping himself to her money, talking her into putting her legal studies aside to put him through law school then leaving her without so much as a good-bye.

But worse than any of that, the Vanessa I knew today had been shaped by her decision to choose Jameson over their baby. Terminating her pregnancy when he'd given her the ultimatum of choosing between him or the baby had been the worst decision of her life. That experience had left such a toxic taste in her mouth that to this day she couldn't respect herself as a woman or allow a relationship to flourish beyond sex or see herself as a mother. It was why she bounced from man to man. It was shy she'd chosen never to have children.

"I chose a man over my child. What kind of woman does that make me? What kind of mother could someone who chooses a man over their child possible be?"

It was why I never passed judgement on her reckless lifestyle. But this path, one that led her to become involved with married men, was one I couldn't in good conscience support.

"I didn't know he was married, and once I found out, I broke it off right away. I told him I wouldn't see him again. You have to believe me, Natalia."

Although I believed her, all I could manage was an, "Uh-huh."

"I swear to you, I dropped him as soon as I found out. Please don't be angry with me." Her voice dipped to an apologetic register.

I could hear the regret in her voice. Still, it took me some time before I turned to face her. "I'm sorry I reacted the way I did."

"Don't be. I deserve it. And I promise to stay away from the men at work," she said doing her best to sound sincere.

My brows shot up. "You know you don't believe that. You love men too much, and Pax's work is seventy-five percent male. It's a cauldron of temptation for you. All I'm saying is do it…"

"Discretely and with modesty," she finished my thought.

I nodded.

"For the record, I don't think I've slept with half the single men in town. Not yet anyway."

The air briefly hummed between us before I burst out laughing and she joined me.

"More pie?"

Shelving what had happened between us as ancient history—which was the way all of our arguments ended—Vanessa nodded. "With ice cream?"

"No other way to eat apple pie. How about a refill of coffee?"

"I'll get it," she said sliding out of her chair in one swift motion.

Back at the table, Vanessa rested her hand on mine. "You know I don't like to argue with you. You're like a sister to me."

By the way she said it, I felt my own sisterly feelings for her stir and I couldn't help but smile. She was far more of a sister to me than Caterina had ever been. "Ditto."

"Pregnancy agrees with you. You're glowing. I know most pregnant women like to think they do, but believe when I tell you that they don't. They usually look tired and frayed. You pulsate with beauty and energy."

"I love being pregnant, but it's early stages yet. I imagine that when I blow up like a watermelon and my ankles swell up to the size of an elephant's, I'm not going to be glowing as much anymore."

"You may be right. Either way, I'm so happy for you. I know how much you've wanted this. You're going to make a great mother."

"You really think so?" I didn't mean to sound as uncertain as I did. "Listen to me. After all the assurances

I've given Pax about him being a great father, I'm not sounding so sure myself."

"It's your hormones." She nodded, seemingly confident in her assessment. "They're pulling you in every which way. Besides, there's no one who would be a better mother than you. Unlike me, you have all the qualities of being a great mother. You're loving, caring, and protective." Her tone was matter-of-fact, but there was something sad in the words.

"What do you mean unlike you? You're all those things, and more."

Vanessa shook her head, her chestnut curls sweeping her shoulders. "No, I'm not."

"You're a good person, Vanessa. You'll…"

"Eventually change my mind?" she asked, getting to her feet and walking our dirty dishes to the sink. She refreshed her cup only when I refused the refill. She set the pot back on the stove and sat back down, tucking long, toned legs beneath her. "Well, I won't."

I really hated Jameson. I hated that selfish, pathetic excuse for a man for how much he'd hurt her and negatively influenced her life, how he'd molded her psyche, and the course of her life. This was all on him. His egotistic actions had driven her to convince herself that she didn't want to have a child of her own. That familiar ball of anger took form in my chest at the thought of the emotional pain that sonofabitch inflicted on her, which to this day was subconsciously a part of her while he'd gone on with his life, to marry and have children of his own.

"I'm happy being that doting, spoiling aunt all kids love to have. Your gaggle of kids will be calling me Auntie Vanessa, won't they?" Vanessa said, more as a statement than a question, and when I nodded, she couldn't help but smile. "All right then, that's settled. What do I have to do around here to get some food? I think I need to offset the infusion of sugar with something salty."

"Where do you put it all? How does an omelet sound?" I asked getting to my feet.

She nodded without a second thought. "It sounds perfect."

Crossing the kitchen to the refrigerator, Vanessa's anxious voice cried out behind me. "Natalia, you're bleeding."

Ten

DAYS LATER, THE words still didn't sound real as Dr. Mann's words played out in my head over and over. "I'm sorry, Natalia, but you've suffered a miscarriage."

Dr. Mann's matter-of-fact tone still ground on my nerves, and the ache of loss rushed at me steady as strong as a fist in the gut.

Although I couldn't understand how I could feel such a sense of loss for something I never really had, I did. That feeling, along with the overwhelming pain and sadness, stayed with me for days and unbeknownst to me I would carry it for the rest of my life.

I couldn't shut off the thought of our lost baby out of my mind, and the nagging feeling that I had caused the loss was inescapable. The notion hovered over me with a crippling hold on my already vulnerable state of mind like a snake on its prey. The baby that had been inside my womb protected against the world, growing and alive, had died because of me. Everything I had done had caused my baby to cease to exist. I hadn't eaten as healthfully as I should have. I hadn't exercised enough. I should have done this or I shouldn't have done that. The excuses sounded irrational even as I uttered them, but my mind was racing to justify the devastating loss that had plagued my life for which I believed I was to blame.

No matter how many excuses I came up with, in the end it was me, me, me, who'd cause the loss of my baby. My body was broken. Aside from the inane comments, "It's part of nature," or "Miscarriages are extremely common," there were no forthcoming answers to what had happened. I felt as if I were being pulled down into dark turbulent waters of despair, deeper and deeper, with no bottom in sight.

I remember faintly hearing Pax's voice as he posed myriad questions to Dr. Mann, and his exasperated breath when he received no concrete answer why I'd suffered the miscarriage.

I felt even more broken then.

Why did it have to happen to me? What had I done to deserve this?

I remember leaving Dr. Mann's office with Pax by my side, his hand wrapped around mine, feeling immensely depressed.

On the way home, with Pax holding my hand, I wept for my baby, and for me.

NEEDING TO RETREAT FROM REALITY, I spent the next few days in bed. Retreating didn't make the pain gnawing at me go away, but it made it bearable.

When I was awake, I spent every moment wondering, asking myself questions that couldn't be answered by anyone.

Why me?

What have I done to deserve this?

Why would God do this to me?

How could I be pregnant one minute and not the next?

What did I do wrong?

I wondered if it was a boy or a girl I'd carried inside of me. I burst into tears at the thought that I'd never know.

I wept for what felt like an eternity.

When I cried out the shock out of my system, I slept, not a peaceful sleep, but a fitful and disturbed one filled with dark dreams.

I became numb to everything around me. Feeling led to more heartache and pain, so it was best not to. I laid in bed for hours staring at everything and nothing. Living in darkness, not knowing when night turned into day, was how my life pivoted from day to day. It was as if time stopped or flew by or flowed at the speed of thick molasses. It didn't matter.

Nothing mattered anymore.

PAX STOOD IN THE BEDROOM DOORWAY, eyeing the untouched tray of food with concern.

"Sweets, you have to eat something. You've lost a lot of blood, and you need to keep your strength up." The tone that would normally have soothed did little now.

"I'll eat something later," I said, but I knew he didn't believe me.

He crossed the room and sat at the edge of the bed. "I'm worried about you."

I knew he was talking about my mental, not physical, state, but I said nothing, simply staring at him with tired eyes.

On the bed I hadn't moved from for days, my arms wrapped around my legs and my head resting on my knees, for a long while we sat in silence. I was certain he could easily detect the tangles of emotions gnawing at my gut.

"I don't know what to do for you, Natalia. I don't know how to ease your pain." His words came out slowly, each one a drop of despair and my heart ached for him. As much as I wanted to give him assurances, tell him that I would eventually rise up and do it every day and a thousand times thereafter, my grief was far too debilitating to make my words sound genuine to him or me. And I remained silent.

I knew silence was selfish, but it was all I could offer then. I couldn't trust myself to say the right things or anything really, for fear I'd break down in tears again.

For a moment, it seemed as if he wasn't quite sure what to say, and he repeated himself. "I'm really worried about you."

"I'll be fine." I mustered a smile that did nothing to appease him.

Pax reached for my hand, squeezed it and latched onto my vacant gaze. "This is not your fault, and we'll try again. Dr. Mann said we could try in a few months. And we will."

He needed my acknowledgement then, so I gave him a muted nod. I wanted to say something else, but I couldn't get the words out. As much as I loved him, and as grateful as I was for how wonderful he'd been the last few days, I didn't want to talk, I didn't want him there. I wanted to cry in darkness for me, for him, for my unborn baby.

I couldn't bring myself to explain to Pax how my grief came in waves and consumed me. I couldn't explain the awful hollowness I felt in my heart, or the wretchedness, or the guilt at having caused the loss. I couldn't voice how this horrible experience crippled and broke me, and that I wasn't sure he or anyone could put it right for me again. He wouldn't understand any of that. I was her mother. It was I who had carried her inside me.

I wanted to be left alone to wallow in my self-pity.

As if reading my mind, Pax tucked me under the covers, shared a kiss with me and left the room, but not before stopping at the door and saying, "Sweets, I love you."

Eleven

PAX POKED HIS head into my darkened bedroom. Since the miscarriage, he'd moved into the guestroom to give me my space.

"You have visitors, sweets."

"I don't want to see anyone."

"It's Janice and her mother. Janice asked her to bring her by." For a moment, I said nothing. "She really wants to see you." The despair in his voice and the thought of seeing Janice's beautiful, toothless smile unexpectedly reached down deep to where I tried to hide myself and my bitter mood softened.

During the past few weeks I had Pax turn away family and friends, who when finding out about my miscarriage began to trickle to my doorstep bearing platitudes, food or flowers, all gestures that did nothing to ease my pain. As well-meaning as they were, I didn't want to see them. I couldn't subject myself to the endless litany of clichés people were inclined to use, in such circumstances.

"It's God's way of telling you that your baby wasn't all right."

"Your baby is in a much better place now."

"I've had two miscarriages before I had Maxine. And look at her now."

"You'll just need to try again, darling."

"Keep your chin up."

I couldn't allow them to make me relive the worst time of my life over and over by asking me questions or offering advice, which wasn't going to bring my baby back. I even refused to see my mother and sister when they came by. After my refusal to see my mother on her second visit, she resorted to calling Pax from time to time to check up on how I was doing.

Vanessa had known from the onset to stay away. She understood that what I needed now was to be left alone, to grieve in my own time.

But Janice, I knew, wasn't going to ask or say any of those things that would upset me. The thought of seeing the freckled-face little girl actually brought a smile to my face.

"I'll be down in a minute," I said, certain that my response both shocked and delighted Pax.

I got out of bed, washed my face, bundled my hair up into a messy ponytail, threw on T-shirt and jeans, and ten minutes later, I walked into the living room. The room was alive with sunlight and overflowed with flowers from well-wishers that until then I hadn't seen. The sound of birds perched on our linden tree in the front yard in boisterous dialogue flowed through the open window. I could hear Mr. Steward's lawn mower sputtering in the distance as he tried to wind up to life. There was the laughter of our neighbor's children as they splashed in the pool and Mr. Belvedere barking as they encouraged him to jump in with them.

There was life all around me and suddenly I missed it.

Janice rushed at me and wrapped her arms around my waist. "Ith tho nithe to thee you Mithess Reed. We all mith you tho much."

I knelt down so our eyes met. "It's nice to see you, sweetie. And I miss you and the children too."

Her eyes, a rich brandy brown, innocently studied my swollen eyes. Brows frowned in confusion, but she politely overlooked my appearance and said, "My mommy told me you're thad." The simplicity of her words had the tears forming in my eyes, but I blinked them back.

"Janice, honey." Mrs. Smith raised a subtle brow at her daughter.

I shook my head at Mrs. Smith. "That's all right. Go on, sweetie. Tell me, what's on your mind."

Hands clasped behind her, she shifted from one foot to the other. "I want you to thelebrate my birthday with me. I want you to come to my party tho you don't have to be thad anymore. Wyatt and Tania are coming and all the other kids too right, Mom?" Janice looked over to her mother for confirmation.

Mrs. Smith nodded. "That's right, honey."

"And we all want to thee you and make you happy. Will you come to my party, Mithess Reed? I'd really like you to come."

Janice's words touched me deeply and made me realize that I'd been hiding in darkness, from life, for long enough. I decided then it was time to move on and celebrate the joys of life. "I wouldn't miss it for the world, sweetie. I'd love to celebrate your birthday with you. Thank you so much for inviting me."

"Oh, you're welcome." She flashed me a wide, gapped smile.

The inexplicable powers of a child's smile, I thought, when it breathed life into me and I suddenly felt weeks of sadness, pain and ache wash away.

"Will you help me make thome decorations for my party, Mithess Reed?"

"I'd love to. We'll work on it on Monday in class. We can get all the children to help us. Would you like that?" From the corner of my eyes, I could see hope written on Pax's face.

Janice gave me an enthusiastic nod "Can we make a paper chain like the one we made at Chrithmath? All in different colors. Mommy can hang it in the back yard. It's going to be a barbecue pool party."

I matched Janice's smile. "We can do anything you want, sweetie."

Pax brought out cake and ice cream, a glass of milk for Janice and a steaming mug of coffee for Mrs. Smith and me. I hadn't eaten well in days and I gladly took the offered food and drink. I devoured it all, and without asking, Pax cut me another piece of cake and refilled my coffee.

Janice and her mother visited with us for half an hour. Never leaving my side, my toothless wonder animatedly filled me in on the goings-on in my classroom. At the end of their visit when Mrs. Smith brushed past Pax on their way out the door, I thought I saw him mouth a silent thank-you.

PAX CONFESSED LATER THAT EVENING TO setting up Janice's visit in the hopes of getting me out of bed and out of the depression, I'd succumbed to. And I was grateful he had.

Keeping my mind occupied and keeping busy was the best therapy. I stopped dwelling on my loss. I sank into my teaching. Getting back to my classroom and children was exactly what I needed, and spending time with Pax and the children, at Janice's birthday party revitalized me and made me realize I'd made the right decision by getting on with my life.

I sank into my teaching, and volunteered to spend two hours after school with Timmy, who was falling behind on his reading. Over the summer break, I offered to babysit Marsha when her mother, who had been diagnosed with breast cancer, required two late afternoon sessions of chemotherapy at the hospital and had no one else she trusted enough to watch over her daughter. And when Tina asked me to take over her summer camp classes, after her boyfriend decided at the last minute they should backpack through Europe that summer, I jumped at the chance.

As busy as I kept during the day, I set time aside for Pax. Spending as much time with him as I could in the evenings and on weekends to rekindle the closeness and the intimacy into our married life was imperative. We took short walks, indulged in romantic dinners, went to the movies, or simply cuddled up on the couch in the solarium talking and watching the stars. Pax never spoke about the miscarriage, not unless I wanted to, and after a few weeks, I never brought the subject up again.

Twelve

AUTUMN'S SWEET BREATH chilled the air, and chrysanthemums in jewel tones were in full bloom. Beyond the kitchen window, trees were aflame in a riot of rust, copper and reds and the leaf-covered ground was a sea of fiery colors. I took the view in, and for a moment, I painted a vision of my little girl laughing and running through the yard, the leaves on the ground crunching under her feet as she chased her dog, Doodle.

I wondered if the vision would ever become a reality. I wondered if I'd ever get a chance to hold her, to feel the pride and sadness as I watched her walk into her classroom that first day of school. Would I ever experience the excitement of helping her get ready for her prom, for her college graduation, or on her wedding day?

The images stayed with me until the front doorbell chimed into my thoughts.

Drying my hands on the white, lace apron, I rushed to answer the door.

"Jesus! Keep your pants on. I'm coming," I shrieked as I rushed past the foyer, and as quickly as I opened my mouth to blast out the oaths circling in my head I closed it.

"Really, Natalia, is that any way to greet your guests?" my mother asked nesting her trademark Dior sunglasses in the golden bob, which was as honey-blonde today as it had been when I was child.

"But you were ring…"

She interjected. "I've taught you better than that."

"I'm sorry, Mom. I was…" I stumbled through the words, then let the sentence hang, realizing that no explanation was going to be adequate for her and when the falsely lashed green eyes slid to the apron with the wet splotches, I rushed to untie it.

"Much better." She subtly nodded her approval.

"Please come in."

The lips, perfectly traced in Dior peach lipstick, pursed. "You look tired. Those circles under your eyes aren't becoming, dear."

My shoulders, as they always did when she was around, hunched as an act of—surrender? Contrition? I never really knew why, and it didn't matter anymore. I was so used to it that it came as an automatic reflex. And as was always the case, I apologized and wondered why I did so.

"Umm, how are you?" I said with a feigned bright smile.

"Don't overdo it, dear. Remember the hair at the back of my neck." She air pecked me and at the thought of rolling my eyes, as if reading my thoughts she said, "No sense in rolling your eyes either, dear," and then proceeded to peel her gloves off one finger at a time, in that sophisticated way the women in the black and white movies did.

Only my mother could make glove removing a sensual act, I thought. I'd often wondered why more of that sensuous femininity, a trait that was inherently part of my mother's genetic makeup, was passed only to Caterina, who, because of it, was the daughter I could never be.

"I was making myself some tea. Would you like a cup?"

"That would be lovely." She settled into the living room couch. "Would you like some help, dear?"

It was safe to assume the offer was an empty gesture, and I declined. The last time my mother had done anything as undignified as boil water was... My memory didn't seem to go that far back.

It took a few minutes to get water boiled, and with tray in hand, I joined my mother in the living room. Eyes darting to the tray I set in front of her, she scrutinized my presentation. I guess the gold-rimmed Tiffany along with the biscuit I laid out in the decorative way she expected passed inspection, because no criticism followed. I didn't dare tell her I'd drained my tea from a white mug into the Tiffany cup.

"How are you, dear?" My mother daintily laced her tea with milk, added sugar and ever so delicately stirred. God forbid the spoon clinked against the cup.

"I'm well." I offered her a biscuit in the graceful Miss Manners way she expected. She smiled at that, seemingly pleased that the etiquette lessons she'd forced on me as a kid hadn't gone to waste.

Reaching for the biscuit, she set it down on the edge of her tea plate. "And how is Pax? I know your father's been keeping him busy with this land deal he's trying to acquire from the Demon brothers."

I stifled the laugh she wouldn't have been pleased to hear. "It's the Diamond brothers, Mom. And Pax is well. He's at the office right now working on the paperwork for the meeting in New York with the brothers at the end of this week. Pax enjoys working with Daddy and Blake."

"I can see Pax wanting to be mentored by Blake Stanton." She said the name almost reverently. "He is a man of breeding and education."

I couldn't deny that the Stanton name opened doors, and Blake had done that for my father. Blake's money had allowed my father to achieve tremendous success in the land development business. Although my father's connections and first-hand knowledge of the construction business had contributed substantially to Stanton & Rossi Developments' growth, my father couldn't have done it without Blake's money, which had been made the old-fashioned way—he'd inherited it from daddy. But to elevate the Stanton's to god-like status as my mother always did was a bit much to swallow.

"Daddy is also knowledgeable," I was quick to remind my mother, who had a tendency to put Blake Stanton above my father.

"Of course he is, darling, but you must admit that Stanton and Rossi reached the level of success they have because it bears the Stanton name. I will forever be grateful to Blake for partnering up with your father. And now that Michael is joining the firm, they have nowhere to go but up. Imagine having two Stantons to contend with. Michael's already making great strides and making his mark in the company. Mark my words, Michael will take Stanton and Rossi Developments to great levels." Eyes beaming with pride lifted to mine for acknowledgment.

I gave her an assenting shrug because she expected it, not because I agreed with her. Michael was the son-in-law that Pax never would be. Although Pax had progressed in his career, was ten times the caring, loving man Michael would never be, Mom had made it perfectly clear she wasn't impressed with Pax. The fact that Pax didn't come from money, wasn't blue blood, or hadn't been educated in an ivy league school, as Michael had, were sure to be her top reasons.

"Yes, Pax has told me about Michael's…unique management style." I wouldn't dare tell her that at Blake's request Pax had "discretely" taken over many of Stanton & Rossi's land deal negotiations, which would have normally been handled by Michael due to his ineptitude. Hard facts would have been wasted on my mother who thought Michael was capable of walking on water.

I didn't completely blame my mother for her blind idolization of Michael. He was a charmer, with the startling good looks that knocked the wind out of any woman and blinded them to his true character. At over six feet with glacial-blue eyes set in a perpetually tanned face framed by a cascade of flaxen waves, Michael never failed to seduce the female eye with blatant male arrogance. It was a primordial quality I didn't find appealing, but women like my mother and Caterina lapped it up. That Michael had chosen Caterina for his wife above the long line of women hoping to lure him to the altar was a privilege my mother to this day prized.

"Michael works hard, maybe more so than anyone I know. Caterina tells me he puts in long hours, seven days a week. He's certainly devoted to Stanton and Rossi. He's been an absolute godsend to your father, not to mention your sister."

Let me jot that down, I thought, because it wasn't as if I'd heard that prideful rant a thousand times before. "How is Daddy?" I asked, desperate to change the subject.

"Your father is fine. He's golfing this morning, which is all he does since he's semi-retired. I don't know exactly what that means, semi-retired. But honestly, the man is obsessed with golf."

I refilled her empty cup, before giving her the opportunity to chastise me for letting her go empty. "Maybe you should try it, golfing I mean."

My mother winced at that. "I think not."

I offered her another biscuit, which she waved down. I always wished I had her discipline with food. "You may enjoy it and you'll get to spend time with Daddy."

"I'll stick to my tennis, thank you. It's a far more civilized sport. Besides, I already spend enough time with your father. I'm glad he's getting out of the office now and taking more time for himself." She lifted a brow when I reached for my third biscuit and down it went back on the plate.

"I'm glad Daddy is taking it easy, he deserves it. And Pax is grateful for all the legal work Daddy and Blake have passed his way." I was about to elaborate on the significance of Pax bringing in the Stanton & Rossi account worth millions in billing to Roth & Associates, but the look on her face told me we'd exhausted the topic.

Leaning back on the couch, she crossed toned legs, paused for a moment. "How are you feeling? Are you fully recovered yet?"

After my miscarriage, my mother had been incapable of discussing it in detail. Avoiding the conversation at all costs. In time, I came to the realization that it wasn't because she didn't know what to say or how to say it, but it was because she couldn't deal with the reality of one of her daughter's being "damaged."

"As recovered as I'll ever be. We've passed the grace period, so Pax and I will be able to try again." To my surprise, her face brightened.

"And are you?"

"Pax and I haven't talked about it yet." I hesitated for a moment, then absently said, "I think I may be ready," surprising myself.

"That's wonderful, darling. I'm so happy to hear because I've come with news of your sister."

"Is she all right? What's happened? What is it, Mom?"

"Caterina is pregnant," she said with a beaming smile.

"That's wonderful news," I said feigning excitement.

As happy as I wanted to be for Caterina, the resentment grinding in my stomach wouldn't allow it. I didn't understand the begrudging feeling that washed over me for my own sister, but it did. She was having the baby that I couldn't. Jesus, when is this going to end? I thought to myself.

"Isn't it just, dear? Your sister is carrying a Stanton. I hope that it will be a boy. That's what Michael and the Stantons are hoping for. They've already come up with the name they would like to call him. Michael William Stanton, II." My mother went on, oblivious to my roiling emotions.

"Roman numerals do elevate your status in life," I whispered under my breath.

"What was that, dear?"

"I said, is that what Caterina wants?" I put in sarcastically to remind my mother that Caterina was a part of the family and the process.

If she heard me, she dismissed the comment. "He'll be called Will. Sounds so regal, doesn't it? Just imagine it, dear, your sister is having a Stanton. There will be regal blood flowing through that boy." Delighting on the idea, she sipped tea with a smile and I didn't dare remark that there was a fifty percent chance the baby may be a girl.

"Why didn't Caterina tell me herself?" I asked when the thought occurred to me.

She crossed toned legs. "Caterina thought...We all thought it would be upsetting for you. It's not, dear, is it? Because this is wonderful news for both families."

"It's not. I'm happy for Caterina and Michael." I was, but somehow the words felt like a lie.

Ostensibly relieved by the outcome of our conversation, she exhaled a breath. "I'm so glad. Caterina found out three months ago, but she wanted to wait until now to say anything. She didn't want to upset you." I found my hand held in her firm grip.

Caught by surprise by my mother's uncharacteristic physical contact and the kind words, I lapsed into a momentary stunned silence that stretched into minutes when she rose and strolled away into the kitchen to refresh the water in the teapot.

Thirteen

Vanessa

THE MOMENT THE young nurse entered the waiting room Natalia felt the shiver run down her back.

"Is Vanessa okay? Where is Dr. Steward? We haven't heard anything in hours." Pax bolted to his feet before Natalia did.

"I'm Mary, one of the nurses caring for Ms. Roberts. Dr. Steward has been in surgery for the past three hours, and before that…well, we've been run off our feet all night. The bad weather combined with the icy roads has resulted in a number of serious car accidents." In white scrubs, her chestnut brown hair tied back in a smooth ponytail, she looked the picture of efficiency.

"Can we see Vanessa?" Natalia asked.

Mary smiled warmly. "I'm here to take you to see her. Please follow me."

Tom, Pax, and Natalia did. The three followed Mary through a series of hallways, past doors, past the nurse's station, and into the I.C.U. It was now six a.m., and the floor pulsed with activity as nurses dashed in and out of rooms, dispensing medication and checking on patients.

Doctors made their morning rounds. A woman moaned out in pain, begging for relief as a nurse explained that she would need to check with her doctor before increasing her dose of morphine. Errant smells, along with the aroma of unpalatable food flooded the floor.

Mary led them to the last room on the ward. "Here we are."

Walking into Vanessa's room, Tom, Pax and Vanessa stopped in their tracks, their feet feeling as if they were nailed to the floor. Vanessa looked like an experiment from a science fiction movie. Attached to her lifeless, ghost of a body was a spider web of tubes and wires. Machines, humming and beeping, monitoring and infusing life into her, were all around her. They heard the rising and falling hiss from the oxygen machine as it pumped air into her.

Natalia's mind slid into a gray mist of despair, and her limbs went limp. A numbness fueled by shock and panic came over me. Seeing the woman she remembered so full of life, silent, and unresponsive to the world was one of the most difficult things Natalia had had to do. For a long while, all she could do was stare. Looking at Vanessa made her eyes swim.

"Jesus, she's…"

"Going to be fine, sweets." Pax took Natalia's hand and pat it calm, and only then, was she able to gather her courage to cross to Vanessa, moving quietly, each step weighing heavily.

Sidling to Vanessa's bed, Natalia bent down to brush a kiss on her forehead. She felt cold, withdrawn, so very silent, and so very small.

"Can she hear us?" Tom asked Mary as she went about checking Vanessa's blood pressure, her temperature, and I.V. bag.

"Yes, we believe so, and we encourage family and friends to talk and read to our comatose patients. I'll give you some privacy. If you need anything, please don't hesitate to ask." She tweaked the IV tube, and turned to leave.

"But we have so many questions," Pax called out.

Mary stopped at the door. "I'm sorry, but you'll have to direct them to Dr. Steward," she said and continued on her way.

"She looks so…lifeless," Natalia said taking Vanessa's limp hand. "We're here, Vanessa. Pax, Tom, and me are right her with you, and we'll be right here by your side until you come out of this. You need to fight. You will come out of this," Natalia told her with a confidence she didn't feel, and as she did, Tom's strangled voice called out.

"Something's wrong. She's breathing all wrong. She's not getting enough oxygen," he said and watched Vanessa gasping deeply, desperately inhaling for oxygen her injured body starved for.

Fourteen

I SAT ON the steps of my back deck and took in the natural beauty that October turned out. I'd always loved everything about fall. Leaves in gold and russet, lemon yellow and apple red that set trees aflame in color and eventually pirouetted to the ground to sculpt the vibrant carpet beneath my feet always left me breathless. I even enjoyed the pungent peaty smell of damp earth that came before an autumn rain as it did today.

"Can I join you?" Pax asked poking his head through the French doors. When I nodded, he crossed the deck to sit beside me on the steps. He'd discarded his suit jacket and tie, and had unbuttoned the first two buttons on his shirt. I caught the faint scent of his cologne and male sweat. "It's beautiful out here, isn't?"

"It is." The air held the faintest chill, and I wrapped my hands around the warm coffee cup.

He was about to wrap an arm around me, but stopped mid-way.

Although I had gotten on with life, I still carried the pain of my loss with me, and our intimate life—as desperately as I'd tried to rekindle—had been non-existent. The absence of closeness between us had created a thick wall of awkwardness between us. Each of us digging into a vocabulary of polite words that skirted the distance, the coldness, the loneliness between us.

Nothing he did or said was right. Nothing he did was appreciated. The kind gestures he made went unacknowledged. Yet, he never gave up, and although I loved him for that, I never told him so.

Although Pax didn't allude to it, I was certain it was why he had talked me into joining him on his business trip to New York. I also knew that his reasons had nothing to do with sex, and everything to do with bringing us back together, with making life flow once again through the vein of our lives as it once had. Still, I wasn't entirely sure I was ready, but the way he'd asked had made it impossible to turn him down.

If truth be told, the crashing weight of loneliness, one I'd left behind when Pax came into my life, resurfaced. Although Pax and I were sharing a bed again, it had been a long while since we shared a heated night together. I'd been tempted several times to reach over to him for emotional and physical comfort, but I still couldn't bring myself to do it. Whether because I didn't feel worthy of Pax's attention, or because I hadn't completely detached myself from the depression brought on by the loss of my baby, or…or…or… The reason was anyone's guess. And as time passed on, I drifted farther away from the need for intimacy.

It never ceased to amaze me how one event, emotionally and psychologically, scarred me so drastically, and how the trickle effect from it became so far-reaching. I was affecting not only my life, but also Pax's, and everyone around me.

I'm not sure how I got to this point, but I was there.

"Would you like me to get your shawl?" he asked.

"I'm fine, thank you." I hated the banality of our conversation.

"I see you're all packed up."

"I am." We weren't leaving for a couple of days, but I began to pack days ago, hoping to get used to the idea and to try to muster the same excitement as I sensed in him.

The conversation with my mother came to mind then, and I thought about the comment I'd absently made to her about being ready to try for another baby, and I hoped to God this trip was the turning point. I needed this. I wanted to let go of my anger for my sister's pregnancy. Caterina, and certainly my niece to be, didn't deserve it.

"I'm looking forward to the trip, Pax."

"Are you, sweets?" His voice rose a pitch.

"I am."

Slowly, he ran a fingertip along my jaw, and when I didn't pull away, he slid his fingers under my chin, pinching as he lifted my face until our eyes met. "Me too."

I thought then, that even though we hadn't made love in so long I'd never seen a flash of anger or disappointment on his face. Reflecting on his understanding, support, and patience during the past few months, I was suddenly conscious of everything he'd done for me, and how little I had done in return. He had been my rock since the miscarriage. He had been there for me at every turn, night and day, with a smile on his face, caring for me, loving me. I thought of how much I'd pushed him away, and that the more I did, the closer he got.

I didn't think it possible, but just then I fell deeper in love with him.

The feelings that had been dormant all these months were now restless and dying to burst free. I rose to my feet and I held out a hand for his. The dazed, look came with surprise and a momentary stunned silence. "Are you sure about this, sweets?"

That he would ask made my heart swell with love. Nodding, I reached for his hand and led him upstairs.

OUTSIDE OUR BEDROOM WINDOW JAGGED STREAKS of white cut through a sky thick with black clouds. I chained arms around Pax's neck, pressed my body intimately to his. The heat from his body seeped into my bones and made my blood beat thick. I felt the blinding need as potent and edgy as the sky thundering above us exploding in me.

"I've missed you."

"I'm…"

He pressed his lips to mine. "I wanted you to know."

I leaned into him and skating my fingers over the front of his shirt, I began to unbutton it. His scent rich and virile intensified as his flesh heated.

Beyond the window, lightning flashed in a brilliant shock of white, and, for the briefest moment, the room exploded with light. Seconds later, a chilling rain broke from darkness and came down in sheets. Its steady drumming against the window gave an exotic feel to the moment.

Pax's fingers trailed up and down my back, and I felt dozens of nerve endings explode in unison. My heart hammered when his hands slid under my T-shirt. His fingertips seared my skin when they skimmed over my breasts, and sparked the long-extinguished flame. I felt a desperate need for him to touch me, to feel his naked body pressed against mine. I wanted to feel him in me, and I whispered the words ripe with longing and need in his ear.

Eyes, turbulent with emotions, full of want, and love met mine. "I've missed you so much."

A lance of lightning exploded with defiance and lit the sky. Rain lashed against the window, fast, furious, and steady.

"I've missed you too."

His mouth met mine with a crushing blow, to take, taste, feast. I felt his hunger, sensed his need burning in the kiss. The jolt from the kiss and the taste of his lips left me breathless. Need, desire, want made rushed fingers fumble to loosen buttons, unsnap pants. The groans of pleasure erupting from our lips when heated flesh met heated flesh melded with the sound of rain beating against glass.

Scooping me into his arms, Pax carried me and lay me down on the bed. The air redolent with the smell of rain and wet earth, Pax kissed me, and the warmth of his breath on my skin made me realize how much I'd missed him. How much I needed him.

I wanted all of him, all there was of him. I wanted to feel him deep inside me. I wanted him to take me and make me his.

His name escaped my lips in a breathless whisper, and there, with the sound of rain pattering on the window, he made love to me. His mouth, tongue, and hands reclaimed me as his. He loved me so sweetly, touched me so gently, and when he slid in me, months of repressed emotions and tension buried deep inside us erupted. Our hearts linked like key and lock, months of suppressed feelings flowed along with our passionate words of love to one another.

Our bodies damp and glowing, we moved together to the tempo of our body's demands. Together in torrid pleasure we moved, with long, slow strokes, clinging, holding, holding until we were ripe to burst. With the thunderous boom that rolled overhead, swamped with love, together we soared and leaped off the edge of the world.

We made love a second and then a third time, and each time the love we shared became stronger, deeper. Captured in his arms, breathing his scent in, I fell into a contented sleep.

IT WAS NINE P.M. WHEN I woke. The rain had stopped and a layer of darkness with stars as clear as glass had settled in. The sense of solitude and peace was deeper than I'd ever known.

I rolled over to face Pax and kissed the lips curved in contentment. "Are you hungry?"

"Mmm-hmm," he said between the butterfly kisses he skimmed over my nose, my cheeks, my neck.

"I'm talking food, Mr. Reed."

He pulled me in closer to him, and I slipped my legs between his. "I wasn't."

"I'm starving."

"The story of my life. I rate below food. I'll order a pizza in a minute."

"Aww, double cheese please."

Pax laughed at that then, he tucked a strand of hair behind my ear. "How are you feeling?"

I traced his chest with my fingertip, letting it cruise through the dark mane. "I feel wonderful. I'm sorry that I've been...distant these past few months. Thank you for being so patient with me."

A gaze of complete understanding fell on me. "I love you, and there's nothing I wouldn't do for you."

His words filled me with the purest form of joy, and I felt my throat tighten. "You know I love you and I love being with you, I just…"

He silenced me with a kiss. "I know."

I looked up into the blue eyes full of love. "Pax?"

His fingers lazily traced my breast leaving a tingling sensation in its path. "Yes, sweets?"

"What would you say if I told you I'd like for us to try again?" Although the question was vague, I knew he understood its meaning.

"Are you sure?"

I could see his eyes deepened in concern, wondering why, after I'd just surfaced from a depression that had taken a hold of me for months, I wanted to get pregnant again.

"I am. I really am. I know the miscarriage took a lot out of me, and I'm sorry I put you through so much, and although I still don't completely understand why I reacted the way I did. Not really. I want to try again. I need to."

He pinched my chin and brought my face up to his. "You didn't put me through anything. You're the one who suffered the physical pain and the emotional scars. Although I was there and suffered the loss right along with you, it was you who endured it firsthand. And I can't even begin to imagine what that must feel like. It's that I…worry about you."

"I know, and as much as I thought I'd never want to get pregnant again, I do now. I feel physically ready to do so and as emotionally prepared as I'll ever be." I hoped my assured tone would win him over.

"If that's what you really want."

"It is, but I want you to also want it."

His expression softened. "You know I want children, but more than that I want to you be happy."

"Trying for a baby will make me happy."

"If it's what you want, then it's what I want also. I want to make sure you're...all right with it."

"I am." I shared a kiss with him, and although he smiled, I could see the flicker of worry in his eyes.

Fifteen

OUR FLIGHT LANDED at JFK on schedule, and we took a taxi to the Waldorf Astoria. Although ominous clouds threatened rain, New York was alive with the everyday bump and grind on its streets. Sidewalks were a sea of rushed New Yorkers, and the streets were a flowing river of yellow taxis, their horns feverishly blaring. Street corners teemed with vendors. A jungle of glass and concrete dominated the skyline, and signs of growth and progress were conspicuous in the scaffolding perched everywhere.

"I'm glad you came with me, sweets." Pax took hold of my hand and squeezed.

I turned from watching New York crawl by our cab window to meet the smiling blue eyes swimming with renewed hope. "So am I. We're going to have a great time."

"I have tickets tonight for Guys and Dolls, and before we head off to the show, my assistant made reservations at Delmonico's. It's the place to eat when in New York. Tomorrow and Sunday are wide open, so we can do whatever comes to mind. We can do some sightseeing. Maybe visit the Empire State Building, or we can take a boat ride to the Statue of Liberty or…" He went silent when I caught him off guard by playing my lips over his.

Thrilled to feel a rush of desire and need for him I leaned into him and whispered, "Maybe we can do something more…fun."

"All right. Once I'm done with the Diamond brothers, I'm all yours."

I enjoyed seeing him flustered. "I'm all yours too."

"I can't wait." Pax tucked a strand of hair behind my ears, as he'd done a thousand times before, but this time there was an exotic feel to his touch. "What's on your agenda until I finish up with the Diamond brothers?"

"I thought I'd do some shopping. A girl can't come to New York and not shop."

"How about once you're done draining our bank account, you meet me at the Diamond brothers' building? We'll plan our evening from there. How's that sound?"

"Sounds like the perfect plan."

"Hungry?"

"Starving."

Pax paid the driver and gave instructions to the door attendant to have our bags sent up to our room. "We can grab something to eat in the hotel restaurant before I head upstairs to prepare for my meeting."

"Sounds good to me."

His hand settled on my back, we strolled through the double doors of the Waldorf. Pure old-world luxury, the hotel was as stunning as it was charming. Columns rose majestically to ornamental ceilings and brass ran in vivid contrast to gleaming Sienna marble and artful mosaic floors. Polished tables groaned with enormous bouquets of red roses with white spray that speared from painted stone urns.

Regency chairs with dark wood trim and gold cushions sat tall and majestic throughout the floor.

Skirting the thronged lobby, Pax and I headed for the restaurant where a young woman with smooth, ebony skin locked long-lashed saucer-sized eyes on us. Pax held up two fingers, and she led us to a table by the roaring fireplace, its heat caressing us like an ethereal, romantic dream. We ordered two glasses of red and the special of the day—sea bass with zucchini flowers.

"When does Michael get in?" I asked when the server set off to place our order.

"I don't know. In the few times we've traveled together, Michael has never told me his itinerary or stayed at the same hotel as me."

This was news to me. "Never? Why not?"

Making a noncommittal sound, Pax shrugged his shoulders.

"Why do you think that is?"

"He just doesn't, Natalia."

Although there was always polite repartee between Pax and Michael, it wasn't difficult to sense Pax's deep loathing for the man. Michael wasn't a palatable human being, but I was never sure why Pax felt as he did. I sensed there was something he wasn't telling me.

"Why doesn't he stay at the same hotel as you? Pax?"

"This is only suspicion on my part, but…" His lips pressed tight together when the server approached our table to set wine glasses down.

I watched him take a long drink then, absently proceed to tap his fingers against the wineglass. "Pax, please finish your thought."

When my mouth drew open again, he blurted out, "I think he's having an affair."

An uneasy silence hummed between us as I processed this bit of information. "Are...are you sure about this?"

"I'm not. That's why I haven't mentioned it. He's very discreet about it, seems to know exactly how to...contend with the situation."

My mind was hazy then, but I understood the veiled implication. "What would lead you to think so?"

"It's a gut feeling, Natalia. Remember, I work in a predominantly male environment where this is an ongoing thing. You learn to read the signs."

"Jesus! Are you saying he's an expert philanderer? That this is an ongoing thing for him. Who's the bastard sleeping with?" I lowered my tone when Pax gestured me to do so.

"I don't know who he's involved with or even know for a fact that he is, Natalia. I don't know any of the answers to your questions. It's my gut feeling. And you shouldn't say anything to your sister. This is none of our business."

I stiffened at the remark. "What do you mean it's none of our business? It's my sister he's screwing around on." The clamor of silverware against china and the voices of patrons and waiters reciting the day's specials began to irritate me.

"Natalia, I don't have facts to back up my suspicions. And you know how Michael is revered by your mother and sister. They're not going to believe you unless we have concrete proof, which I do not. The last thing I want is to destroy a marriage based on assumptions."

He was right, of course, but my gut feeling told me Pax's instincts may not have been far off the mark. I'd always suspected Michael to be the type of man who wouldn't think twice of denigrating his vows, my sister, and family. "God, I knew his sense of morality was tenuous, but I didn't think he was so lacking in integrity."

When I remained quiet, lost in thought, Pax said, "I shouldn't have mentioned it." He ran his fingers down my arm until our fingers linked. "Please don't let it spoil our weekend. I want our time in New York to be as memorable as the past few nights."

"I won't allow Michael to spoil our weekend. I'm sorry you've been burdened with this."

"I'm sorry I brought it up." I watched Pax lift the glass to his lips and take a long contemplative sip. "I never told you this, and I shouldn't be saying it because it's completely unprofessional of me. I managed to talk your father and Blake into giving me complete signing authority for all the deals I negotiate on their behalf." When my brows creased in confusion, he explained.

"Since your father and Blake are relaxing their grip on the business and unwilling to travel, Michael has become a signatory officer for the company. Meaning, I do all the legwork, and he simply shows up to sign off on the paperwork. It's the only reason he attends the meetings with me. But I got so sick and tired of his ego and the way he arrogantly flaunts his name at every meeting, demanding a respect he hasn't earned. So through, let's call it creative means, I talked your father and Blake into giving me signing authority. Part of me did it for professional reasons, but mostly because I needed to take him down a few pegs." When I cocked a brow in admiration, he misread it as rebuke and quickly said, "I would never put Stanton and Rossi in harm's way."

"That never crossed my mind." We went silent while the server set our food on the table and warned us about how hot the plates were. "So why is he here with you on this trip?" I asked once she'd moved on.

"I guess Blake hasn't gotten around to telling him yet." Pax reached for the salt and pepper, sprinkled both over his sea bass then, flaked a piece onto his fork. "My guess is he's delaying it because he doesn't want to deal with the repercussions."

"Repercussions?" I watched him chase his sea bass with wine.

"Taste the sea bass. It's delicious." He gestured and I did, but made a rolling gesture to speed him along. "Diana Stanton. From what he's told me, Diana won't be pleased when she finds out her little boy has essentially been discharged from running the company. Blake's already banned him from interfering at any of his other companies. Diana's the only reason why Michael's working at Stanton and Rossi."

"Family drama can be draining. Safe to assume my sister knows nothing about this?"

"No, and you can't say anything about it."

I read lawyer-client privilege into the comment and nodded. There was something so dubious and unfair about having to keep everything I now knew from Caterina. My own sister. I eased my guilt by telling myself that if I did say anything to her she would likely dismiss every word as a jealous fabrication on my part. "I'm sorry you have to deal with so much." I wished I could do more than apologize.

"One plus is that the Stanton and Rossi Developments account and all the other business Blake has turned over to me is worth millions in billable hours, and it was enough to…" Pax stopped abruptly.

I detected something in his voice, a flicker of concern in his eyes. "Enough to what?"

Pax waved our server over and ordered two more glasses of wine, leading me to believe we were both going to need them. Once she left our table, he turned to me. "A few weeks ago, I was offered partnership in the firm." He scrutinized my expression, as if trying to gauge my reaction.

A crushing sadness struck me, and I looked up at him. The tears trembling along my eyelids spilled, and he reacted with the panic that men tend to at the sight of a woman crying.

"I didn't mean to upset you, sweets."

"I'm sorry. I'm so sorry." My stomach felt raw and edgy, and the tears now flowed faster.

Pax waved away the approaching server with drinks in hand and nodded his assurance to curious diners that everything was fine. "You're sorry for what? What do you have to be sorry about?"

"For being solely focused on myself. For not recognizing what was happening in your life. The fact that I'd trivialized such an important event in your life is inexcusable." He deserved better.

Pax swiped tears from my cheeks with his thumb. "You've had a lot going on. I didn't want to bother you with this."

"It's no excuse. I should want to revel in your successes with you. And I would have, had I not been so selfish."

"You're certainly not selfish. You've gone through a traumatic event, and you just needed some time to deal with it."

"You making partner is fantastic news, Pax."

"You're okay with me making partner?"

I signaled the server to bring our drinks.

"Of course I am. I'm so proud of you. The fact that you've been offered this opportunity is a significant achievement. And you so deserve it. You've worked hard for this." I raised my glass to meet his.

He took a quick drink with me before resting his hand on mine. "Are you sure you're okay with this? I didn't think you'd welcome the news."

The remark took me by surprise. "Why would you think that?"

"Accepting this partnership means longer hours, weekends, and a lot more travel. I didn't want to take time away from you."

There was something in the way he said it that touched me deeply, and I thought that there couldn't be a more perfect man than him.

"Is it what you want?"

He shrugged his shoulders. "It's what I've been working toward."

"That's not what I asked you. I asked you if this partnership is what you want. What you really want." I squeezed his hand, encouraging him to say what was really on his mind aloud.

This time, Pax didn't hesitate to answer me. "It is."

"Then you should accept it."

"But it'll mean that I'll have less time to spend with you, and I don't want to do that to you right now." His genuine concern for me reflected on his face made me realize he was a far better man than I'd ever imagined.

"I'm sorry. I'm sorry that I've made it so you feel guilty about acknowledging something that you've strived so hard to achieve. This is about you. For once, I want you to think of yourself."

He slowly traced fingers across my face. "Do you have any idea how much I love you?"

"I think I do."

Sixteen

BY LATE AFTERNOON, a rolling darkness hovered over the city, and the threat of rain loomed in the air. That didn't put a damper on my planned shopping trip to Fifth Avenue. At Armani, I bought two suits—one blue, and the other black—with skinny pants, perfect for work. I walked out of Saks with a pair of black pumps and a pair of patent slingbacks, each with matching totes big enough to carry my textbooks. I window-shopped at Tiffany, although I was tempted by the shiny stones, the earrings, the bracelets, and necklaces displayed against black velvet to do just that. I almost handed the sales clerk my credit card when she showed me the gold teardrop earrings. Guilt had me holding back.

As much as I loved the allure of the beautiful stores on Fifth Avenue, the need to see Pax overtook me and I cut my shopping spree short. Armed with my bags, I hailed a taxi and gave the driver the address to the Diamond Developments' building in the Garment District.

As the driver wound the taxi through the maze of one-way streets, I eyed the scene of a hurried New York that played outside my window. Even under gloomy skies, sidewalks were crowded with New Yorkers and tourists, their heels clicking on concrete as they rushed to and from. It felt exhilarating. This was definitely the city that never slept and I was thrilled to be there.

Pax and I were ordinary people leading ordinary lives, but in New York, nothing seemed ordinary. Life, excitement spurted inside me, and it felt like the beginning of something good and right. Although I still didn't know what was to come, I felt now as if I could face it head on. Being in New York with Pax, felt like a turning point.

I felt confident about life, about getting pregnant again and having the baby we wanted. I felt the flutter in my stomach at the notion. It was a great feeling to again feel sure about my and Pax's future, to feel as if I had a hand in our destiny.

"Stop the car," I cried out.

When the driver pulled the taxi over, I followed the woman on the sidewalk ahead of me with my eyes. She carried a Victoria's Secret bag in one hand, and her smoky dark hair bounced over the shoulders of the white camel hair coat. The confident, sensual swing of her gait screamed Vanessa, and I could swear the woman who stepped into the St. Regis hotel was her.

We hadn't spoken in a few days and neither of us knew the other's plan for that weekend. Wanting to surprise her, I jumped out of the taxi, and I followed her into the hotel. Making my way through the tall glass doors, I scanned the lobby, but I couldn't see Vanessa anywhere. I checked the bar and the restaurant. Both were crowded with a collection of sophisticated, well-dressed men and women enjoying, what I assumed, were perfectly aged whiskeys, brandy, and cognacs, or sophisticated drinks that were shaken not stirred, and meals prepared by Michelin starred chefs. I thought of my mother then. She would feel right in her element amongst these people.

I didn't spot Vanessa in the crowded bar or the restaurant, and I crossed polished marble to the curved reception desk.

"Could you please ring Vanessa Roberts' room?" I said to the young man behind the counter who produced a particularly charming smile to great effect.

"I'm sorry, ma'am, but there is no guest by the name of Vanessa Roberts registered with us," he informed me after checking the guest register.

"Are you sure?" Next to me, a couple from Texas stepped up to the counter and gave their check-in information to the desk clerk. Their toddler eyed me with large brown eyes, and deciding I posed no threat, waved at me. I waved back and playfully stuck my tongue out netting myself a giggle.

"I'll check once more," the clerk said and the little girl and I carried a stick-out-the-tongue contest while he scanned the register.

"No, no one by the name of Vanessa Roberts registered with the St. Regis, ma'am," he said after his thorough check.

"How about Tom Webster," I said hoping she and Tom were on an on-again weekend trip, which periodically happened—mainly when Vanessa needed T.L.C.

"Sorry, ma'am. No guest by that name either," he said with an apologetic shake of the head.

"Thank you for your help." Waving to the little girl, I turned to leave, and at that moment, I caught sight of Michael stepping off the elevator.

He wore a black suit, gray silk tie, and a matching shirt. His honey-brown hair perfectly in place, he looked unapologetically handsome, rich, and virile. His mouth was curved, whether sulking or smirking was difficult to tell. One thing was for sure, he donned the expression of sexual gratification on his face—or so I thought.

I should have guessed he would be staying at the most expensive hotel in the city. "Hello, Michael." I stood in his way with a look that could have turned him into stone.

His breath caught when his eyes swept over to me. "Natalia. What are you doing here?"

"I'm in New York with Pax, and I was in the area. Is Caterina with you?"

His lips peeled back in a snarl. "No, why would she be? I'm here on business. Besides, you know damn well she's in no condition to travel."

"Then who are you here with, Michael?" My direct question infused with rage caught him off guard and silence reigned. In situations like these an entire twenty seconds of silence was a long time.

Michael fixed what I construed as a hostile gaze on me. "What's your problem, Natalia?"

The lack of instantaneous denial, in my eyes, instantly branded him guilty. "I've heard you don't like to travel alone."

The muscle on Michael's jaw quivered, and I took that to mean he knew what I was insinuating. "Who from?"

I dismissed the question. "Why are you staying so far from Pax's hotel? You're both supposed to be here in collected effort. You're both here for the same meeting." The din of conversation in the hotel lobby mingled with the traffic sound of horns beeping out on Fifty-Fifth Street.

"So, spreading rumors is what that mediocre lawyer husband of yours is resorting to now."

He was dodging. "That sounds to me like the retort of a guilty man."

He shot me an icy glare that could have turned me into an icicle. "I don't have time for this nonsense, Natalia. I have a meeting to get to." He pushed past me then stopped. "And I'm warning you, Natalia, don't go talking this nonsensical gibberish to your sister or you'll have me to deal with." He turned and headed out the front door, and I thought, there goes a guilty man.

THE CONVERSATION HAVING LEFT AN UGLY, metallic taste on my tongue, I didn't want to risk running into Michael at the Diamond office, so I opted to head back to the hotel. From the lobby of the St. Regis, I made a quick call, and left a message with the Diamond's receptionist for Pax to meet me back at the hotel. I then hailed a taxi.

The taxi ride to the Waldorf Astoria took longer than I wanted it to, but once there I headed straight to my room and made a beeline to the mini fridge. Two small bottles of brandy poured over ice, I slid open the curtains to the window overlooking Park Avenue. Kicking my shoes off, I took a seat at the couch facing out the large picture window. The rain New York had been expecting all morning began to fall then and beat on the window in a rhythmic tap-tap-tap beat.

Even after the drink had wound its way through my system, the wave of fury for Michael swelled in me. I felt edgy, and I couldn't sit still. Against my better judgement, I made the type of decision you shouldn't when in an irrational state. I called Caterina.

When she answered the telephone, I led the conversation with a feigned excuse about checking the price for a Prada handbag I'd seen at Neiman Marcus. My call of course had been to tell her about my suspicion of Michael's infidelity, but I'd decided against saying anything when after a few minutes of conversation her tone led me to believe she suspected nothing. Without facts, there was little I could say, and lobbying innuendo about her husband was only going to strain our already rocky relationship. Our talk, as it always did, ended in detached pleasantries.

No use dwelling over something I could do nothing about, or so I told myself.

I shook the conversation from my head, refilled my glass with brandy, and waited for Pax.

PAX DIDN'T GET BACK TO THE hotel until six p.m., and we both opted to stay in. I ordered room service, and twenty minutes later, in front of a flashing display of lightning, thunder, and rain, we ate our Angus hamburgers and fries, and chased it with red wine. During our meal, Pax told me about his successful meeting with the Diamond brothers, which Michael endeavored to sabotage, and I in turn told him about my day. I told him about seeing Vanessa and chasing after her into the St. Regis only to lose her, and then, to run into Michael.

"That may be why he tried to sabotage the deal," Pax said.

"That's insane. This land deal only stood to benefit him." I watched Pax uncork the bottle of Malbec and refill our glasses.

Pax nodded. "I wouldn't put it past him to thwart the negotiations to undermine me and make me look bad. What bothers me is that he put information on the table that only a select few of us had, which ended up costing Stanton and

Rossi two million dollars more. Well, jokes on him because in the end I closed the deal with the Diamond's and the property is now Stanton and Rossi's." He bit into his hamburger.

"What a giant douche. I wish I knew what my mother and Caterina see in him." I bit into my burger, and contemplated how my butt would handle a second one. "After our exchange today, I'm leaning more toward believing he's absolutely cheating on my sister."

"You're not thinking Vanessa and Michael are here together?"

The thought hadn't occurred to me, and the comment shot a brief, but very real chill through me, and I suddenly lost my appetite. I paused, and considered. The idea that Vanessa was with Michael hadn't crossed my mind once, but now it was all I could think of. She wasn't checked in under her name, or was here with Tom, but the number of people she could be in New York with were endless. But no one she knew could possibly afford the St. Regis hotel.

"She wouldn't, not with my sister's husband," I said.

Pax arched one thin dark brow. "I know she's your friend, but…"

When he hesitated, I pressed. "But what, Pax?"

"Vanessa is…shall we say…too liberal and undiscriminating with her partner selection."

"Are you saying she'll sleep with anybody?"

Pax was about to answer me, but in the end shifted an apprehensive gaze to the glass of wine in his hand.

"If you think she's sleeping with Michael, just say so, Pax."

"I don't know that she is. I'm just saying that it's not beyond the realm of possibility where Vanessa is concerned," he said after a contemplative sip of wine.

"She's not like that. I don't believe she would sleep with my sister's husband."

"Sweets, she slept with Bobby Roth, a married father of three who's not only slept with almost every woman on staff, but who, for obvious reasons, would never leave his wife. I'm only mentioning it because I know Vanessa tells you everything, and I'm pretty sure you know about it." His eyes stayed level with mine and his voice was matter-of-fact.

"Yes, I know about that, and I had a chat with her. She won't be doing it again."

"I don't care if she does. It's her life, and what she does is none of my business. I don't like that type of gossip, which has made the rounds in the office, being associated to you."

"I know."

In the silence that followed, the rain, which was now coming fast and hard and pounding the window, lent an intimate feel to the otherwise unsettling moment. I wondered what it was about the drumming pitter-patter sound of rain against a window that could transform your mood.

"Now, let's put all talk of Vanessa and everyone else aside and concentrate on us. We have a baby to make." He smiled as he said it.

Taking my hand, Pax led me to the four-poster bed. With the dreamy sound of rain beating against the window, floating on emotions, he made love to me. Flying with sensations, losing control until the whip of pleasure jolted us together, we plunged over the edge. We made love twice more throughout the night and each time we began to drift into sleep, thoughts of Vanessa and Michael filled my mind.

Seventeen

DECEMBER SWEPT IN, and the days grew shorter. The inevitable freezing chill of an approaching winter stung the air, and thick snowflakes, the first of the season, drifted from a steely sky cloaking the city in white.

Our intimate life was back on track, better than it had ever been, and our encounters became spontaneous and adventurous. They took place wherever and whenever the mood struck. There were no boundaries, no limitations.

It was one of those impulsive encounters—maybe the one in the shower, or in the foyer when Pax got home after work—that got me what I'd prayed for.

I was pregnant.

My heart swelled at the notion that I was again pregnant with our baby. Our baby, I repeated over and over. I loved the sound of it. I felt an overwhelming joy at the thought. Suddenly everything that I'd gone through—the depression, the feeling of defeat, the heartache of loss, the guilt and fear—slid away, faded from my memory as if it never happened.

I didn't see myself as the strong, courageous woman that Pax saw. I saw myself as a woman with such a burning need to have a baby that I'd undergo any physical and emotional pain necessary to make that a reality.

I stole a side view glance of myself in the dresser mirror. Absently, my hands travelled to my belly. Envisioning my belly growing with every passing day, my grin spread from cheek to cheek. Although this wasn't the first time I was experiencing this moment, I nonetheless felt the same sense of joy and wonder I had with my first pregnancy.

I thought of Pax. Giving him the child he'd always wanted thrilled me as it had months ago. I couldn't wait to tell him. I found myself smiling up until the moment he walked in the door.

"Hi." Chaining my arms around him I kissed him, our tongues joining in that familiar rhythmic dance I'd come to love.

"That's quite the welcome. Thank you." Pax set his briefcase down and removed his coat once I unbuttoned it.

"I need to tell you something."

"What is it, sweets? Are you okay? Is everything all right?"

"Everything is perfect," I said guiding his hand to my belly.

"You're pregnant?"

"I am. I was two weeks late and decided to get the doctor to run the test. He confirmed it for me this afternoon."

"That's wonderful news." His face quirked with apprehension, told me differently.

"Is it, Pax? Aren't you happy about it?"

Pax's expression remained thoughtful for a moment. "Of course I am."

"You don't seem happy."

"I am, sweets. I'm just…"

"Concerned for me." The subtle nod spoke volumes. Framing his face with my hands, I looked into the blue eyes full of worry. "I'll be fine, Pax. It's going to be okay."

Eventually, I felt his arm go around my waist. "It will be. How do you feel?"

"I feel wonderful, I really do. I can't tell you how fantastic it feels to be carrying our baby," I said, with the smile I hadn't been able to wipe off my face since getting the test results.

"Sweets…"

When he let his thought trail, I finished it for him. "I promise to keep an open mind this time around."

"I don't want you to get hurt."

"I know, but you understand that I need to do this." My loss was something I would never forget, but I couldn't shield myself forever in my pain and give up on having the child we both wanted.

"I do.''

"All I want is to have a baby. To have our baby, and I'm willing to do whatever is necessary to make us a family."

"I know." Pax lowered his forehead to mine. "Promise me that this time you're going to take every precaution necessary and that includes R&R, lots of it."

"I promise." I brushed my lips against his once, then again to take in the taste of him.

Pax took my hand and led me to the living room. Setting me down on the couch, he settled next to me, and I set my feet on his lap. "That feels great." I purred when he firmly ran his thumbs in a circular motion down the soles of my feet, and sent sheer pleasure through my system.

"You relax while I order a pizza and get the fireplace going."

"You, Mr. Reed, have magical fingers." I purred some more. "And as tempting as your offer of pizza sounds, we can't stay in tonight. We need to get ready for your company Christmas party. We should make an appearance. You're a partner now, remember."

Pax made a funny face that told me he had no interest in spending the night with a forged smile making small talk. "I doubt they'll even notice I'm there. They're expecting close to five hundred people tonight."

"They will miss you. Aren't many of your top clients going to be there?" I tried to be the voice of reason.

A roll of the eyes came before the nod. "You know Vanessa is going to be there."

"I know, but there will be so many people there we may not even run into each other."

"So, you're still ignoring her?" He reached for my left foot, and proceeded to let his magical fingers run up and down.

"I'm not so much ignoring as disregarding her."

"For one, that's the same thing, and two it's been two months since New York. Shouldn't you try talking to her?"

"She didn't once mention her visit to New York when we had lunch a week after we got back. That in itself…"

"Doesn't make her guilty of anything," Pax jumped in. "I'm sorry I put the thought of Michael and her in your head. Why don't you try talking to her?"

"What am I supposed to say? So, Vanessa is it true that you're rolling in the sheets with my sister's husband. That you're letting Michael poke you behind my sister's back."

"I think you can ask in a subtler way." He brushed a gentle finger up and down my sole.

"I could, but I'm not going to. Besides, I thought you'd be happy I was distancing myself from her. I know you've never really approved of Vanessa's lifestyle."

He stopped his hand mid-way up my foot. "I never said any such thing. I wanted her to keep her private life, just that, private and not entangle you in it."

"Well, consider me disentangled. You should fire her."

"Fire her? You're the one who talked me into hiring her, and now you want me to fire her?" He continued his massage of my feet when I flexed them at him.

"That's exactly what I want you to do. She's betrayed me. And you know that was she not my friend that's exactly what you would have done when you heard the rumor about her and Bobby Roth."

"That's not so. I don't particularly like her loose lifestyle, but she's one of the best paralegals we have, and an asset to my department."

I tore my foot loose from his grasp. "I can see I'm not going to get anywhere with this conversation. May as well go and get ready for this party of yours."

"You go ahead. I'll be up after you're done with your shower. And, sweets?"

"What?" I stopped short at the door.

"R&R."

"Yeah, all right. And don't get any ideas about trying to mend fences between Vanessa and me. This is between her and me."

He held his hands up, palms out. "I wouldn't dream of getting between the two of you," he said, but I knew Pax well enough to believe he would.

Eighteen

THE HALL HAD been converted into a Christmas wonderland, and the atmosphere was festive in the packed to bursting ballroom of the Royal York hotel. A twenty-foot fir, draped in silver garland, flickering lights, and colorful ornaments, stood at the center of the room. A glowing silver star crowned it. Hundreds of snowflakes, as if suspended on air, fell from the ceiling. Tables draped in green, with red poinsettia at the center and candles in silver holders flickering filled the room. The scents of perfume from women in glittering gowns, and aftershave from men in tuxedos crowded the air.

The Dom Pérignon flowed generously, as did the music with a provoking beat that had couples, filled with the merriment of the season, swaying seductively on the dance floor.

Pax and I plunged into the crowd and weaved our way through the packed room to our designated table. At table fifty-nine, we found Vanessa and Tom, along with Pax's secretary, Nora, and a couple I didn't know, enjoying drinks and nibbling on hors d'oeuvres.

I turned to leave, but Pax closed a hand over mine to stop me. "There won't be any seats available anywhere else."

The disdainful eyebrow I lifted at Pax went ignored, as did my, "You staged this," comment when he turned to take Tom's offered hand.

Tom, who looked particularly handsome tonight in a navy-blue suit against a white silk shirt and a merry cherry-red tie, pecked me on the cheek and proceeded to pull out the chair next to Vanessa for me. I had no choice but to accept it.

Introductions made and greetings exchanged, I heard Pax whisper to Tom, "We better get out of the line of fire," and both made a beeline to the bar.

The air was suddenly crowded with a collective cheer from the room as Elvis Presley's baritone voice launched into his famous Blue Christmas rendition.

"You look good," Vanessa finally said breaking the thunderous silence that lingered between her and me.

"You do too," I said back.

Her body was squeezed into a black Fendi dress that left little to the imagination. Her dark hair flowed in long thick waves over her shoulder, above her eyes long, thick, dark lashes fluttered, and her lips were painted a fiery red.

An awkward silence stretched out between us, and I could feel Vanessa's eyes studying me. Minutes passed before she opened her mouth again to say something, but she quickly shut it when Caterina and Michael emerged from the crowd and walked to our table.

Caterina and I exchanged a look of surprise. "I didn't know you were coming tonight."

"I didn't either. It was a last-minute decision on Michael's part, and since I could really use a night out, I gave in. You know, dress up and feel glamorous for a night. I'm so sick and tired of being pregnant, and sitting around getting fat, and feeling ugly," Caterina said and as I looked her over, I wondered why she would make such a ludicrous statement.

At five months into her pregnancy, you wouldn't know she was carrying a baby in that tiny tummy, and tonight she looked stunning in the strapless, teal silk. Yet as beautiful as she looked, Michael barely acknowledged her, and I had yet to see them utter a word to each other. It terribly saddened me. At a time when Caterina should be glowing, she was anything but.

"You look beautiful, Caterina," I said, and as willing as I was then to offer more praise and a listening ear, I didn't offer either. I knew she'd rebuff my words, and never open up to me about her and Michael.

"Thanks," Caterina said brushing the honey-blonde locks that spilled loosely on silky, smooth shoulders back, and taking the farthest seat from me.

I turned eyes on Michael, closely watching the interaction between him and Vanessa. The deliberate, slow intimate survey he gave her caught my attention.

"Did you arrange for Michael to sit at your table?" It came out of my mouth before I realized the idea was in my head.

Vanessa's eyes narrowed at the raw accusation. "No, why would I? How could I? I had no input in tonight's seating arrangements."

"That's never stopped you before."

Vanessa's jade eyes deepened in color. "Did you ever think that maybe Nora did it?"

"Why would she?" There was no way that Michael would ever be interested in Nora. As brilliant as the woman was, she was ordinary, with drab hair, thin lips, and was neither the feminine nor the soft type of woman Michael liked.

"Maybe because he's eyeing her like he wants to jump her bones right there."

I slanted a look at Michael, who to my surprise was casting an eager eye over her.

"Yeah, no way. A good attempt at a diversion on your part though." I snarled.

"What's your problem, Natalia? I want to have this out."

"You do, do you?" I hissed low enough to not attract attention at the table.

"Yeah, I do." Vanessa hissed back.

"We need to do this away from prying ears." I bolted to my feet, and she followed.

"Fine by me," she said and followed me to the lobby, and out the front doors of the hotel.

"You've been an absolute bitch since you got back from New York and I don't know why." The words came the moment we stepped out into the wintry air.

Snow, thick and light, floated weightlessly from a matt, dark sky, thick with stars. The sidewalks and roads were gray with slush, and windshield wipers were whipping at the highest to wipe off the fall of snow from cars moving at a snail's pace.

"Really, you don't." My huffed breaths rose in puffs of white.

"Jesus H. Christ, Natalia, if I knew I wouldn't be asking." The snow spitting and fluttering all around us drenched our dresses and our hair. "What's bothering you? What did I do wrong?" A stiff wind slapped us and Vanessa blew on her hands for warmth.

"You were in New York the same weekend I was. I saw you at the St. Regis." I waited for a response.

"Oh, Jesus." Vanessa began to pace, whether for warmth or out of guilt I couldn't tell.

"I saw you. I chased after you to surprise you, but I wasn't quick enough and I lost you in the crowd."

"I didn't know."

"You didn't want me to know. You didn't want me knowing you were there with him."

She wrenched her hands, and nipped at her bottom lip.

I suddenly felt a bone-deep chill and I wrapped my arms around myself for warmth. "How could you, Vanessa?"

"I know, I know. I didn't tell you because…well, because I knew you wouldn't approve." The wind whipped snow on her face, mascara stained her cheeks black, and her eye shadow became smudged. She was starting to resemble a Jackson Pollock painting.

"You think? I want nothing more to do with you, Vanessa. We're no longer friends."

"Don't say that. I made a mistake. I'm sorry, Natalia. I promise to put an end to it." Black tears spilled down Vanessa's cheeks.

"Are you kidding me? Regardless of how frayed my relationship with my sister is, she's still my sister."

"But… Wait, what's your sister got to do with this?"

"A lot, considering she's Michael's wife."

"And what's Michael got to do with any of this? Oh, no, no, no," she said after a short contemplative pause. "I wasn't there with Michael. I was there with Bobby Roth."

I stood there, watching her, with the snow falling on her hair, dusting her bare shoulders. "You weren't there with Michael?"

"Of course not. I would never do that to you. He's your sister's husband. But more than that, it's...ewww, Michael. The man is a narcissistic, arrogant asshole. I don't know who would be attracted to that. Oh, sorry." Vanessa scrunched her face, and whether from the relief that washed over me or from the ridiculous way she looked in her make-up stained face I couldn't help but I burst out laughing, and soon enough she joined in.

My face wet with tears and snow I said, "I'm sorry. I should have known better."

"Yeah, you should have. You know I'd never do anything to hurt you. And as for Bobby..."

I stopped her there. "No, no, we're not doing that now. I'm already drained enough as is."

She nodded. "You do look...something. I wouldn't say drained, but there is something different about you."

"Yeah, it's this wet hair dripping, make-up running down to my face look I have going right now," I said running my fingers through my limp hair.

"There is that, but that's not it." Vanessa tossed back her snow-covered hair as she studied me. "I can't put my finger on it, but..." She paused to give it some thought, and it took but a few seconds to hit her. "Oh, my God! You're pregnant, aren't you?"

Eagerly I nodded. "I found out this afternoon. I picked up the phone one hundred times to dial your number."

"Forget that. You're telling me now. I think I'm going to cry. I know how much you wanted this. I'm so thrilled for you."

"You have to keep it quiet. Pax and I don't want anyone to know, not until the time is right."

"Mum's the word. I'm beyond excited for you."
Vanessa giddily took me into a wet embrace. "What's
wrong?" she asked when I went quiet.

"I'd never admit it to Pax, because he worries too much
about me, but I'm scared of what may happen."

"I know you are, but nothing is going to happen. Are
you listening to me? Nothing."

I nodded, and wished I could shake the nagging worry at
the base of my skull.

Nineteen

Vanessa

VANESSA'S BREATHING STABILIZED; we were asked to wait in the waiting room for Dr. Steward. It was two hours later when she walked into the waiting room. Lab coat, over brown slacks and a tan shirt flowed behind her like a superhero's cape. Tom, Pax, and Natalia had been assured she was one of the country's best neurologist, and now seeing the intelligent hazel eyes behind the black-framed glasses, and the discernable confidence radiating from her, Natalia believed it. She was tall, with a face washed in the hardships of her profession, and although her peppered hair was in desperate need of brushing, her movements were precise and elegant.

Natalia bolted to her feet. "How is Vanessa, doctor? Is she okay?" "Please have a seat." Dr. Steward gestured everyone down as she sank into a chair. "I apologize for the long wait, but our main concern right now is taking care of Vanessa. I want to assure you that my team and I are doing everything we can for her. That being said, I'm sorry to have to tell you that Vanessa slipped into a coma after her last seizure."

The words came at Natalia like a bullet, fast and sharply. The air clogged her lungs and she gasped for breath. "A coma? But how can that be? Tom said she was seizing when he last saw her. How can she go from having seizures, which she's never had before, to becoming comatose?"

Though Dr. Steward looked directly at Natalia, Pax and Tom listened in. "People who suffer traumatic brain injury don't necessarily show immediate symptoms. The injury Vanessa experienced at time of impact unfortunately progressed into swelling in the brain. The swelling increased the pressure inside her head, and prevented blood passage to her brain causing the continuous seizures, and ultimately the prolonged unconsciousness."

The room went eerily silent as they processed in shock.

"How long is she going to be in a…this state?" Tom asked when he got his voice back.

"I'm sorry, but I can't pinpoint a timeframe for you. A patient in a comatose state can last days, weeks, months or, in isolated cases, indefinitely." When Natalia's brows raised in dismay at her vagueness, Dr. Steward said, "Please rest assured that Vanessa is in good hands. She's getting the best care in the country, and we're doing everything to decrease the intracranial pressure, which is now our major concern, as is—"

"As is what, Dr. Steward?" Natalia's stomach bunched into a tight knot when Dr. Steward stopped long enough to read her buzzing pager. "Is everything okay?"

"I'm sorry, but I need to get back." Dr. Steward kept her expression bland, her voice mild as she bolted to her feet, but Natalia couldn't help feel a jolt of panic.

"What's wrong?" Natalia rose on legs that had gone weak to chase after Dr. Steward, but Pax took a hold of her arm and she fell into him.

Twenty

PAX LED ME to the living room where a crackling fire, with embers glowing and twirling in fiery dance cast the room in long shadows. The coffee table was draped in red. At the center, a solitary red rose speared out of a white vase, and white candles flickered bright. All around us, Dean Martin's baritone voice flowed declaring Amore. It was our second Valentine's celebration, but far more special, because today we were celebrating it as a family of three.

After plating pizza and pouring himself a glass of red wine, and me cranberry juice, Pax pulled out a neatly wrapped box. "Happy Valentine's, sweets."

"But I didn't get you anything. We agreed no…"

Pax lowered his hand to my belly. "You got me the best gift. Go ahead open your present."

"All right." My eager fingers slipped off the white bow and tore the red paper to expose a velvet blue box. When I snapped it open, a gold mother-and-child pendant with a diamond sparkled at the center of white satin.

Pax clasped the necklace around my neck. "You can add the baby's birthstone later." There was a fist around my heart, squeezing so tight. "You like it?"

My fingers traced over pendant. "It's beautiful. I love it, thank you."

We spent the rest of the night designing the nursery.

I made notes, jotted down on paper our mutual decision to paint walls in canary yellow, with colorful monkeys, elephants, and giraffes stenciled throughout. This was a difficult decision to make since Pax insisted on a fiercer collection of animals: tigers, cheetahs, alligators and snakes, which I believe would result in years of psychiatric care for our baby. The window overlooking the conservation park would be draped in white, not green—as Pax suggested— and for baby's entertainment, we planned to hang a merry-go-round light fixture, not a spaceship. I didn't dare veto his suggestion for the large built-in bookcase deciding I would use it to display the baby's toys.

When we were done exchanging ideas, Pax poked the fire and added more wood. Settled on the rug next to me, he tugged me closer. "I'm certainly glad I had a say in our baby's room design."

I laughed at that. "You had some great suggestions."

"Mmm-hmm."

"Hey, you're getting the bookcase, aren't you?"

"You'll thank me when our child turns out to be an avid reader and prodigy with the highest grades in school." He let his eyebrows rise above the blue eyes reflecting fireside fire. "Are you happy, sweets?"

"I'm ecstatic," I said kissing him.

He kissed me back with the same flowing emotions. "I'm glad."

When he deepened the kiss, and parted my lips with his tongue to nip, and to tease mine into a slow seductive dance, I felt the flutter in my stomach. His mouth hot and hungry now, raced along my throat, back to my mouth. I felt his heart beating fast, his body pulsing with need. The heat from the fire intensified as did that of our bodies.

The moment seemed dreamlike and all I wanted was for him to take me there and then. I wanted him inside me. With that thought, I started to undo the buttons on his shirt. My fingers found his bare chest and I felt his silky, smooth hair between them. When his mouth found its way up to my ear, he whispered words ripe with love, desire, and need. He lay me down close to the fire and slowly kissed every part of my body, nibbling his way down, thrilling me. He did so methodically, passionately, and like the conductor of a beautiful symphony, he drove me into a swelling crescendo of cried delight, my fierce moans, and whimpering sounds filling the fire lit room.

His body hard as steel pressed against mine, he plunged into me. I watched those blue eyes swimming in emotion as he rose and fell. Joined with him, riding the wave with him, he held on for as long as he could, and when he could bear it no more with a sobbing moan he told me he loved me and on a shudder, he let himself go.

It was the perfect conclusion to a perfect evening.

THE SMELL OF COFFEE, BACON, AND eggs wafted into the living room when Pax, barefoot and shirtless, jeans hanging low on his hips, walked in with a breakfast tray in hand.

"I made you breakfast." Pax set the tray down and joined me on the rug imprinted with our bodies.

"Thank you, but I'll have coffee for now. Decaf?" I waited for his nod to add sugar and milk.

His hands brushed tangled hair away from my face. "You should eat something. You're eating for two now."

"I will. What time is it?"

"It's ten, but it's Saturday and you're allowed a sleep-in." Pax lazily traced a fingertip down my arm.

"Are you going into the office this morning?"

"Nope, I'm staying right here with you. We can sit in front of this fire for the rest of the day if you want."

"I want," I said, my eyes flickering to the dancing snowflakes outside the window. I'd always liked the way snow transformed everything into a powdery, white splendor.

"It's been snowing all night." Leisurely, his fingers worked their way to my breasts, his thumb caressing my nipple sending flashes of pleasure.

"It has. I'm going to take a shower. Would you like to join me?"

"Yes, please," he quickly piped up, with an eager look that made me laugh.

"I thought you would." I threw off the comforter Pax had covered me with, and it was then we both saw the stark red stain against the ivory rug.

Twenty-One

WHEN THE KETTLE whistled, I poured water on the tea bag and added milk and sugar. Hot cup in hand, I threw a shawl over my shoulders and stepped out on the front porch. Ankle-deep snow hugged its edges, and icicles as sharp as the biting cold that hit my face and seeped deep into my bones hung from gray slate.

It was six a.m., and the world was hushed with dawn, almost dreamlike, as an early morning snow drifted lazily and transformed everything in its path into crystalline white. On the horizon, shafts of light from a rising sun cut through a darkened sky, painting it crimson and gold and I thought how life went on regardless of the disappointments that filled your life. The sun would come up tomorrow as it would the day after and the day after that.

I heard the door behind me creak open. Pax stepped out and draped my coat over my shoulders. "It's cold out here," he said, rubbing the chill out of my arms.

"I'm sorry if I woke you." I felt his arms chain around my waist.

"I worried when I woke and didn't find you next to me. Are you okay?" Pax nuzzled his cheek against mine the feel of his stubble against my skin was familiar and comforting.

Letting hot tea slide into my system I watched a car pass by, snow crunching beneath its wheels, wipers furiously swinging to keep up with the onslaught of slush. "I'm going back to work Monday."

Pax's hands released their hold on my waist and. "Are you sure? You've only been home a few days."

As much as I wanted to hide from everyone and everything, I decided I wouldn't, not this time. I didn't make the decision for my benefit, but for Pax's. I couldn't run away from the sense of loss, but I promised myself I wouldn't drag Pax into that whirlpool of pain and despair all over again.

I lifted my gaze from our joined hands to meet his eyes. "I'm sure. I need to keep busy."

He looked into my eyes as if wondering if he should talk me out of it, but in the end, he seemed to decide against it. "All right, if you're sure."

I nodded, and as much as I tried to hold my composure, Dr. Stein's words rushed at me. "I'm sorry, Natalia. Tests indicate you've suffered another miscarriage." The pain sliced deep, and sadness came and I buried my face in Pax's chest and I say, "I'm sorry. I'm sorry to be putting you through all of it."

"You have nothing to apologize for, sweets." He rocked me, stroked my hair.

My sobs muffled against his chest I said, "I do. It's me, my broken body causing all this."

"This is not your fault. Do you hear me?" he said, kissing my forehead.

"It is and I'm sorry. I'm so sorry." My heaving sobs rose in puffs of white vapor.

Staring into my eyes, he used his thumbs to wipe the tears from my cheeks. "You have absolutely nothing to apologize for, sweets." Tucking a strand of hair behind my ear, he said, "I love you, I always will no matter what challenges life throws our way. You are the best of me and I love who I am when I'm with you."

Love flowed through his words, and made my pain, my sadness dissolve. I'd never imagined I could love him more than I already did.

"You need to lie down for a while and rest. The doctor prescribed R&R after your surgery."

"Will you stay with me?"

Nodding, Pax reached for my hand and led me up the stairs. In our bedroom, as my grief insidiously sucked the remaining strength from my beaten body, I stood there as he undressed me and slipped a nightgown over my head. He tucked me under the covers and crawling in next to me, he spooned his body to mine. With his arms chained around me, I cried low, pitiful sobs that echoed in the darkened room.

I don't remember how long it was before my emotionally drained mind and exhausted body floated into the first restful sleep in days.

I WENT BACK TO WORK THE following Monday. I stayed as busy as I could. I didn't spend the endless hours of reading through mounds of library books, in the hopes of finding the elusive answers to why what had happened, as I had with my first miscarriage. Surrounding myself with my children helped take my mind off my loss, myself, and in time, the shock of my miscarriage waned. The fact that no one but my parents, Caterina, and Vanessa knew of our loss also contributed to my recovery. Keeping well-meaning friends and co-workers in the dark helped Pax and I work through our grief on our own terms, in our own time.

There were still times when I spent longer than necessary in the shower or went for long walks to have a good cry. I was certain Pax knew exactly how I spent those long absences, but he never questioned me. He understood that as much as I needed to heal with him, I needed to grieve on my own.

"Mithess Reed, Mithess Reed," an excitable Jenny called out.

"Jenny, you know you need to raise your hand and use your inside voice." "Thorry, Mithess Reed, but my hand ith buthy holding my toof. Thee?" Jenny opened her hand for all to see the discarded tooth.

"That certainly is your bottom tooth." When the children oohed and ahhed in admiration, Jenny returned a toothless grin, making everyone giggle. "What do we say to Jenny, children?" I led them in the song we'd written for such an occasion.

> *Congratulations, Jenny, on your new tooth.*
> *We're all happy for you.*
> *When it grows in, make sure to brush it,*
> *In the morning, in the eve, and after*
> *Every time you eat,*
> *So that your smile always looks lovely and sweet.*

Her tooth wrapped in tissue, I set it in her lunch box. "Make sure to show it to your mommy and daddy when you get home."

Jenny nodded diligently. "Don't forget the note to the Toof Fairy, Mithess Reed."

"We would never do that, sweetie, would we, children?" I looked to the children, who were already nodding their assurance to a worried Jenny. "All right then, shall we get to work on composing Jenny's note to the tooth fairy?"

Jenny let out a sound that was distinctly childlike, and the all too familiar deep-seated ache reached deep into my heart.

Twenty-Two

THE RINGING OF the telephone startled me out of a deep sleep at three a.m. The metallic taste of panic in my throat, I answered it on the second ring.

"I'm sorry to wake you, Natalia. I wanted to let you know that Caterina's water broke and she's been rushed to Mount Sinai." My mother's voice sent a shiver down my spine.

"But she's only into her eighth month. Is she all right? Is the baby okay?" I sat up in bed, my agitated movements made Pax turn towards me with a drowsy, questioning look.

"They say they're going to have to perform a caesarian." At the end of the telephone line, my mother's voice sounded strangled.

"What do you mean she didn't gain the proper amount of weight?" My question garnered a defeated sigh from my mother. "She wasn't eating well? Jesus Christ, when did the doctor tell Caterina she was undernourished? Did no one think to insist she change her diet?"

"I'm sorry, Mom. I'll apologize to God at first opportunity," I pledged to my mother, a devout Catholic who hadn't set foot in church in years.

"I know how hard-headed, Caterina is, but you should have…Diana and Blake just got there?" I covered the receiver and relayed the information to Pax as my mother went off on a nervous tangent at the end of the line. "What about Michael, is he there?" I asked when Pax mouthed the question. "He just got there? He didn't ride in the ambulance with Caterina? Where the hell was he?"

I apologized again when my mother made it clear she didn't appreciate that type of language.

"Why did it take so long to track him down? What do you mean you couldn't find him? It's three in the morning, where the hell was he?" I regretted the harshness of my tone even as the words came out. "I know you're just his mother in law, but… All right, Mom, I know he's not your responsibility… Calm down, Mom … I'm sorry. I didn't mean to agitate you… Mom?" I pinched the bridge of my nose. "Yes, I'm done with my pontification. Make sure Michael stays by Caterina's side… Mom? … Of… of course I'll be there as soon as I can. Try to calm down, okay, Mom," I managed to say before she hung up.

Pax took the phone from my hand and replaced it in its cradle. "We better get you to the hospital. I'll drive."

PAX AND I FOUND EVERYONE IN the waiting room on the fifteenth floor of Mount Sinai's maternity ward. An unnatural silence cut between them like a hot knife through butter. Stoic and composed Blake Stanton idly thumbed through the sports section of the day-old newspaper. Next to him, Diana, looking as if she'd stepped out of her weekly salon visit sat with a woolen bucket hat nestled in the silvery-blond hair swept back from the perfectly made-up face. She was seemingly engrossed in an article in the glossy Vogue in her hands. My mother, the epitome of proper etiquette around the Stanton's, forced my father and herself to fall into their poised composure. From the number of empty cups on the table next to her, she was on her third coffee and fidgety hands subconsciously tore at the lip of the Styrofoam cup in her hands.

Formal greetings exchanged, Pax and I fell into the silence, and anxiously awaited Michael's update who now by Caterina's side as the doting husband and excited father-to-be, would wander into the waiting room to give us an update on her condition.

"She's being rushed in for an emergency caesarean section. The baby's under distress, the oxygen supply is being compromised. Also, Caterina's blood pressure is dropping." The words said in one quick breath, before he ran out of the waiting room leaving my mother drawing out the words to her many questions.

"She's in good hands, Mom. She'll be fine." I did my best to gloss over the heedless rush of anger I felt for Michael who although was playing the concerned husband role to perfection now, I blamed for my sister's poorly state. It was presumptuous of me, but I stopped trusting him from the moment Pax told me of his suspected infidelity and tonight's disappearance act made me a firmer believer of his philandering ways. He was probably on top of his slut the entire time Caterina was at home struggling to deal with the confusion and distress of an early labor.

I had to marvel how Caterina couldn't know or even suspect what Michael was up to. The man wasn't home at three in the morning. How could you not know or care where your husband was and with whom? If she did know, why put up with it all? How could she disregard her self-respect, and blatantly sacrifice her baby's wellbeing? Was money, and a life of privilege, worth it?

I turned to my mother whose feigned composure was draining her. What she would have preferred to do at that moment was walk off the anxiety, or bark orders to the medical staff, anything other than sit there in the passive, controlled way she was. I wondered whether she had any inclination of Michael's cheating. After all, your mind had to jump to conclusions when your son-in-law wasn't in bed next to his wife in the middle of the night. I considered mentioning my suspicions to her, but I had no proof.

I wondered if Diana or Blake knew of their son's philandering. Was Michael mirroring what he'd seen at home growing up? They do say we become our parents.

I closely studied Blake's face, trying to read the eyes set in a handsome face framed with a mast of thick, silver hair and creased with few lines—a product of a privileged life. Blake's eyes looked innocuous enough. That may have been because he was sitting next to Diana and she had never seemed to me like the type of woman to put up with any nonsense from anyone, let alone her husband.

Watching them side-by-side, Diana at fifty and Blake at fifty-seven, made a formidable couple. Diana was a few inches shy of Blake's six-foot frame. She was slim, with sharp hazel eyes, full lips, which I was certain were collagen infused. Her face was preserved to a youthful forty through the medical wonders of Botox. She was an icy woman, who put decorum above emotion, and I wondered if that had possibly driven Blake into the arms of other women and now his son was simply imaging his father's actions.

Michael's voice cut into my thoughts when beaming with a prideful smile he appeared to announce the arrival of Michael William Stanton, II. Assuring us that mother and baby were well, Michael went on to explain that Will, weighing a mere four pounds two ounces—for precautionary measures—was to remain in neonatal care until Dr. Rosenberg felt satisfied his weight was within a reasonable range.

Watching my face, Pax linked his fingers with mine. "Are you all right?"

I nodded with a smile of reassurance. "I'm an auntie."

CATERINA'S GAZE ROLLED OVER TO PAX and me when she saw us at the doorway.

"Can we come in, Cat?" My eyes scanned the room for Michael. The last thing I wanted was to face him head-on. I wasn't sure I'd be able to hold my tongue and the last thing my sister needed now was me lashing out at her husband.

Caterina looked too tired to smile, but she said, "Of course, come and meet your nephew."

Wandering into the room, my eyes immediately darted to the bundle wrapped in the blue blanket, stubby arms with tiny-fisted hands stretched out from his long slumber as if embracing his new life. Downy dark hair, a tiny pug nose, and large black eyes, which then opened to the world for the first time, stole my heart. He was the most beautiful little thing I'd ever seen, and although I couldn't help but wish it was me in Caterina's place, my love burst through me like bright rays of sunlight.

I felt Pax's hand pump mine in tender encouragement "He's gorgeous and perfect, Cat."

"He is, isn't he?" Caterina, exhausted and without a note of make-up, radiated the glowing aura of motherhood. "Would you like to hold him?"

I eagerly nodded. There was nothing more I wanted than to hold that child in my arms.

"Only for a moment. They need to settle him in an incubator. Will, meet your, Auntie Natalia," Caterina said, settling Will in my arms.

"Hi, sweetie, I'm the auntie that's going to spoil you rotten. I'll babysit you any time you want and take you to the park, and when you get older, we'll travel the world together. Would you like that?" Will squirmed in my arms as if acknowledging my words. "You're tired, aren't you, sweetie? It's been a trying day for you. You wanting to stay put in your mommy's belly and the grown-ups not letting you do what you wanted." Will stretched and yawned, his mouth puckering into a tiny, pink circle.

"I think he's ready to take a nap," the nurse said and unwillingly, I set him in her arms.

At the foot of Caterina's bed, I caught Pax's eyes on me. They were filled with what looked like sadness and pain. I saw then what I hadn't been able to see before. He was hurting for our loss as much as I was.

Twenty-Three

IT WAS TEN-THIRTY when Pax and I wound our way through the silent halls of Mount Sinai to the bank of elevators. Boarding the first elevator to ping, Pax leaned in to me. His arms around me, binding us like Velcro, he took me in for a long, deep kiss.

"What was that for?"

His fingers closed over my hand, he brought it to his lips. "I know how difficult this was for you."

The unexpected comment threatened to shred my already fragile composure and bring me to tears. "I'm happy for Caterina," I said, but I sensed he could see the crushing sensation of shame on my face at the resentment washing over me.

"I know you are. You're an auntie now, and everyone knows you will love that child to death, but you're also human, and after everything you've been through, holding that baby in your arms couldn't have been easy for you."

His words hit so close to home, I struggled to cloak the tangle of emotions he'd stirred and I looked away, fixating an absent gaze to the floor buttons that began to light up in descending order.

Pax's expression softened. "Don't feel guilty for resenting your sister's happiness. It's a human reaction and it will be a short-lived sentiment."

Twelve, eleven lit up as the hot tears burst from my eyes and I whimpered, "But it's my sister. I shouldn't be feeling so resentful," I burst out saying, tasting the wrongness of it in my mouth.

"Do you resent Will?"

"No, no of course I don't. He's beautiful and special, and I love him." Nine, eight the countdown was on as if I was descending into the depths of hell.

"You don't resent your sister for having him, you resent our circumstances. You resent that out of all the random couples in the world, this was thrust on us. Why from all the women who don't deserve to be a mother, or couples who don't deserve to be parents, why God chose us to hurt like this? All those thoughts that overwhelm you with guilt come down to your one flaw, that you're human. There's nothing wrong with feeling the way you do.

Anger, resentment, guilt, and all those other emotions work in concert with love. Like everything else in this life, you can't walk into the emotions store and buy a bag only of love—the best emotion of all. To get love you're forced to buy the bundle, which are all these other nasty emotions you hate feeling. But all those emotions combined are what make you such a caring and loving person."

I turned a blurred gaze to him. "You're disconcertingly wise for your young age."

"I don't think it's a matter of being wise as much as knowing you. You're a strong, loving, caring woman and I'm proud of you." He wiped my cheeks dry. "As I told you before, we'll try again…if you want."

A moment of hushed silence weighed between us. I was glad when the elevator doors opened at the parking lot level and brought a chill with them. Letting the cold air fill my lungs, I stepped out and into the brightly lit parking lot with Pax trailing.

It wasn't until we got to our car that Pax reached for my arm and swirled me to face him. He took my hands and pressed them to his chest, squeezed them as an apologetic gesture. "Sweets, I'm sorry I brought it up."

Refusing to meet his gaze, my eyes drifted to the side, focusing on the bright red lights of a car backing out, its engine revving before it drove off leaving the smell of engine exhausts lingering in the air.

Pax took my face in his hands. "I've upset you. I didn't mean to. I'm sorry I brought it up. I thought you needed to hear it from me."

I eased into my response. "I did. I'm…I'm scared, Pax. What if I have another…and they tell me I can't ever…?"

He pulled me into him and said, "We don't have to do anything you don't want to do."

"We're a couple. Whatever decisions we make, we do it together."

He stroked his hands up and down my arms. "Would it be so bad if you were stuck with just me? Grant it, I drive you crazy when I miss the hamper and leave dirty socks and underwear where they fall. And I know I've caused you many eye rolls when you find that I yet again have forgotten to rinse the sink hair free after a shave, or…well, you get the picture. Would it be so bad being stuck with a pig like me?"

A lump the size of a tennis ball formed in my throat even as I let out a laugh. "I've never ever considered being with you as 'stuck,' but if there is anyone I'd want to get stuck with, it's you." I squeezed his hand and felt him respond in kind.

"I'm glad, 'cause I love being stuck with you." He glided his lips over mine long enough for his taste to slide into my system. "I know it's too soon to talk about it, and we don't have to for some time, but I've been thinking and, well, there are alternatives we can consider. We can talk about it whenever you're ready...or not. I'll leave it up to you."

My heart bloomed like a wildflower under a summer's breeze. Here was love, I thought, unconditional and boundless love. There was nothing he wouldn't do for me.

I knew then that if I lived to be a hundred, I'd never love anyone as I did him.

At that moment, I decided for Pax's sake we would try for another baby.

Twenty-Four

Vanessa

VANESSA WAS NOW in a prolonged state of unconsciousness, unresponsive to her environment and kept alive by a series of machines. The only sign of life in her was the interminable beeps of her heart monitor, the rise and fall of Vanessa's chest, that terrifying green line on her monitor as it ran straight before it peaked and fell.

Natalia wondered where Vanessa's mind was. Was it subconsciously active, and if it was, what was she dreaming about? Natalia hoped they weren't dreadful, jumbled dreams, where the horrible accident replayed in her mind. She hoped Vanessa wasn't seeing her parent's horrible death or that she was at the wheel. She'd blame herself for the rest of her life, Natalia thought, and right now a burden like that wouldn't be conducive to her recuperation. Natalia hoped she was thinking of her and the great times they'd shared together. Natalia hoped thoughts of Tom and the love he felt for her filled her.

They'd told Natalia she wasn't in any pain, and she prayed to God she wasn't.

Lying there so still and quiet made Natalia think of death. She wished it didn't, but it did, and as much as Natalia hated the thought, there was a real possibility that she would die. As much as Natalia wanted to distance herself from the thought, it haunted her.

Looking over at her, Natalia thought Vanessa was just as beautiful in sleep as she was in life. But the silence was deafening. Never did Natalia imagine any room with Vanessa in it to be so eerily silent. Natalia wanted to shake Vanessa, and bring her back to life. When Natalia reached out to touch Vanessa in sleep, she thought she heard her moan. "She will hear everything you say to her." Dr. Steward strolled to the foot of Vanessa's bed and picked up her chart. She wore blue surgical scrubs: hat, gown and shoes, and looked to be in desperate need of sleep.

"Mary mentioned it," Natali said turning to her.

"It would be good for you to talk to her. Let her know you're here. That she's not alone. I'm sorry I haven't been out to speak with you sooner, but it's been a crazy night. A tour bus heading for New York hit a patch of ice on the Gardiner Expressway and rolled into an embankment, and we had to admit twenty patients, seven critical, when St. Michael's Hospital couldn't take them. She seems stable for now," she said after reading Vanessa's chart and looking over the machinery. "I know you have a lot of questions, and I promise to answer all of them, but I'm still waiting on a couple of tests results. I'd like to have them in my hand before I sit down with you and discuss her condition in more detail. Why don't you grab something to eat in the cafeteria?"

"My husband and Tom are there now. I didn't want to leave her alone."

"Vanessa is lucky to have such a caring friend by her side." Empathy rather than the authoritative professional demeanor Natalia had seen earlier shone through at that moment, and she gestured Dr. Steward to the seat next to her. "I wouldn't mind a short rest. I've been on my feet for sixteen straight hours."

"How did you know she's not my sister?"

She creased her brow. "I am a doctor."

"Right. She's been my best friend since…forever. And now, with her parents dead, Tom, my husband and me are the only family she has," Natalia told Dr. Steward.

"I see. I'm sorry." Dr. Steward made a notation on Vanessa's chart, signed off on it.

Out the window, Natalia could see the sun blazing bright in the spread of blue as it rose to replace an outgoing moon. The cape of snow left behind after last night's storm gleamed brilliantly white.

"She's a fighter. Always has been."

"She is that, and strong. The head trauma she suffered was significant. She's lucky to be alive."

"What's going to happen to her?"

"I don't know. We're going to have to take it one day at a time. I realize it's not a scientific response, but medicine is not the perfect science people deem it to be. Particularly when we're dealing with such a unique case."

Dr. Steward response took Natalia aback. "What do you mean unique? I didn't think that comatose patients were all that rare."

"No, they're not, but…" Dr. Steward stopped short. "The tests results I requested on Vanessa should be back in a couple of hours. Once I have them I'll be able to better answer your questions," she said with a straight face, but the hairs shot up on the back of Natalia's neck, which told me there was more she needed to tell her.

"What...what type of tests? What do you mean?"

"Please be patient. I'll be able to better answer your questions when I have the tests results, which I'm hoping to get in the next couple of hours. You should get something to eat. It won't do you or her any good if you don't keep your strength up. If you'll excuse me, I need a change of clothes, and a strong cup of coffee. I promise I'll come see you the moment I hear anything." She strode out the room before Natalia could ask any more questions.

Although the room was warm, Natalia's hands went clammy and cold and she felt the beginning of a throbbing headache working its way in. People's minds weren't made to deal with this type of constant uncertainty, Natalia thought.

Twenty-Five

FROM MY KITCHEN window, I watched Vanessa, her body glistening under a film of sweat, as she detoured from the sidewalk to jog across the green stretch of lawn and straight to my front door.

"Good morning," I called out, stepping onto the porch.

Over the sound of a lawn mower in the distance, the music of birds trilled all around us. Bees buzzed in song as they flitted over the flowers dazzling under the summer sun.

"Hey." Vanessa leaned over, and tried to catch her breath.

I handed her the ice-cold Pellegrino. "It's the middle of June. How you can jog in this heat is beyond me."

"No pain, no gain," she said, holding the bottle against her forehead and neck.

"Shower, then breakfast?"

Vanessa took a long pull of water, and exhaled a, "Yes, please."

"Scrambled eggs and buttered toast okay?" When she nodded, I stepped aside to let her in. "It'll be ready by the time you come down."

Freshly showered, Vanessa walked into the kitchen, filling it with the scent of her lavender soap. "Nothing feels better than a shower after a long run." She dabbed her towel at the stray droplets of water clinging to the ends of her hair. "You need to come running with me."

"I'm not a runner. Swimming is more my pace. It's why I talked Pax into the indoor pool when we did the house reno." I set plated eggs and buttered toast on the table. "So, how was Bali?"

She draped the damp towel on the back of the chair and slid into it. "It was excellent. Sun, white sand beaches, pristine turquoise water and romance wrapped in one package. You and Pax have to put it on your must-visit list." She took a forkful of eggs, then bit into her toast.

"Uh-huh." Across from her, I drew my knees up on the chair and propped my chin on them.

"Tom and I had the most wonderful time. We went scuba diving and horseback riding on the beach. We had dinner by candlelight every night, and for dessert," she flashed a mischievous wink, "we had the best imaginable sex. We did it on the beach, in the pool, in the Jacuzzi…you name it, and we blessed it."

I cleared my throat. "Too much sharing."

Vanessa laughed heartily, and I could see the happiness radiating from her face. "Sorry, but I can't begin to tell you how great it was. I had the best time ever. I love spending time with that man," she sang out, her smile deepening as she reflected on the events.

There was something odd about her. Something I hadn't seen before in her eyes. Then, with gale force, it hit me. "Oh my God, you're in love. And you're in love with Tom."

She laughed a quick bubbling sound of denial. "No, I'm not. I'm not in love with anyone. And don't you go spreading rumors," she said, but there was no mistaking the emotion in her eyes, the enduring smile on her face.

"You are. You're finally letting your emotions show. You're in love, and don't bother denying it."

She gave me a shrug of feigned indifference. "You know that Vanessa Roberts doesn't fall in love or commit to one man."

Dismissing her comment, I folded her into a hug. "I'm so happy for you."

"Stop it, you silly girl. I'm not in love, with Tom or anyone," she said in a weak attempt to convince herself, and me.

"You can deny it all you want, but it's written all over your face. I can see it in the look that comes over you at the mention of his name. I can hear it in your voice."

She faltered, and her expression underwent that transformation of delighted bliss that comes over people in love. "You can see all that?"

"Yeah. I think you've had this wall up for so long, not letting in any man in for fear they'd hurt you like Jameson did, that you can't see it. You should embrace what you feel, how you feel. Bask in the joy of it. This may be the start of something exciting and new for you," I said, hoping she'd embrace the fact that loving someone could be a positive, fulfilling experience.

Vanessa absently toyed with the gold loops at her ears. "You think so?"

"I know so. I've never seen you so gaga over a man before. I'm so happy for you. I knew sooner or later you'd meet that special someone who would penetrate that tough veneer of yours and sweep you off your feet, and love you as you deserve to be loved. And no one will love you more than Tom does."

She tilted a blushing gaze up to mine. "Okay, okay, that's enough about me. Fill me in on what's going on with you."

"There's not much to say really." My shoulders tensed up.

"What's wrong, Natalia? You know you can tell me anything."

In the silence that followed, I pressed my lips together to hold in words and emotions. The tears burning in my eyes, I made my way to the counter, refilled my coffee cup, and remained there aimlessly staring out the window.

Under the spill of sunshine, the grass glinted green, and in the grove, the pines, linden, and maple trees painted the scenery with rich greens and reds. A Blue Jay hopped from tree to tree, stopping only to burst out in song when the four resident squirrels playfully raced across the fence in a straight line.

Vanessa got to her feet and came to stand beside me. By then the tears were streaming down my cheeks.

"Oh, honey." She took my hand and led me back to the table. "Talk to me."

"It's nothing."

"It's not nothing if it's driving you to tears."

"I can't get pregnant," I finally cried out, hating myself for the emotional outburst.

Vanessa wrapped comforting arms around me. "You will. You need to give it more time."

"We've been trying for months now and I don't think I will. And what's worse is that everything has become so mechanical and routine. Everything works around my ovulation time, around schedules. There's no spark to our intimacy anymore. I'm afraid…I'm afraid that I won't be able to give Pax the family he wants and that our relationship has reached an impasse, one we won't be able to mend."

Resolute eyes froze to mine. "You listen to me. Nothing's going to come between you and Pax. You will get pregnant. You need to give it more time." She stood and went straight for the liquor cabinet to get us both something stronger to drink. Replacing the coffee in my hands, with a glass of brandy she said, "Drink this," and fixed an unblinking gaze on me until I did.

"What if I can't? Pax deserves the family he's always wanted, and I have a nagging feeling I'm not going to be able to give it to him." I knew she'd understand how much I wanted that not as his wife, but as a woman.

"You don't know that. And would it really be so bad if it were the two of you?" The blunt question from anyone else would have unleashed a swell of anger in me. "Drink some more brandy."

Under her piercing gaze, I took the last of my brandy. "He said the same thing."

"Well, would it be so bad?" Vanessa poured two fingers of brandy in my glass.

"No, of course not, I wouldn't mind one bit. I love being with Pax. He's my best friend, my soulmate. I could live my life happy and complete with him by my side. But he deserves to be happy. He deserves someone who can give him the family I can't. He deserves a…a complete woman." As the words escaped my lips, I felt something break inside me.

Vanessa's eyes narrowed as a sympathetic anger spit out of them. "I don't want to hear such nonsense from you. For one, you are a complete woman. You're a kind, caring, and loving woman. You're a devoted wife, a wonderful friend, a fantastic, hard-working teacher. And two, you and Pax are meant for one another, and he loves you like crazy."

"And I love him, but love should bring joy, not heartache, which is all I'm doing. He needs a woman who can give him what I can't. I'm thinking of giving him the option of walking away. Giving him the divorce that will free him to search out the woman who will give him the happiness he rightly deserves." My tears ripped through the words, and Vanessa pushed me to take in more of my drink. My throat was so dry I welcomed the smooth, slow burn it offered.

I felt Vanessa's grip on my arms then, irritation on her face. "You will do no such thing. I want you to stop talking nonsense. I'm going to do serious harm to you if you act on this crazy notion of yours." Her tone told me she meant it.

"But—"

"There are not buts." Vanessa's mouth formed a tight line. "What you're going through right now is a… rough patch. I have to admit that I don't understand your deep-seated need to have children, but I do understand that it's what you both want and that you shouldn't give up on it because you've had some…complications. Your bond is strong enough to withstand this bump because he loves you and you love him. Promise me you won't give up on yourself or Pax. And promise me you're not going to blab out this nonsense of yours to Pax."

"He's such a good man. He deserves better. All I want is for him to be happy, even if that happiness doesn't include me," I said, sounding defeated, feeling trapped in a vortex of despair.

"He's the best. I love that man. I've often told you I wish I could clone him. But you're a good person too, Natalia." She wrapped her arms around me. "You deserve him because you deserve to be happy. Besides, it's not that difficult to figure out that he can't live without you."

I sighed, suddenly conscious of my outburst. "I'm sorry to be dumping this on you."

Vanessa's automatic response was, "Everyone needs someone to talk to, and it's best you get it off your chest instead of keeping it bottled up, which is probably what's stressing you to the point of causing your infertility. You're stressing so much that it's preventing you from getting pregnant."

I wanted to believe her, but I wondered if the solution was as simple as that. The more I rolled her remark over in my head, the more I saw the wisdom in it.

"You're probably right."

"Not probably. I am right." Her imperious tone put a smile on my face and loosened the knot of tension in my stomach. "Now, I'm going to reheat my eggs and refill our glasses. I know it's early, but a few glasses of morning brandy never hurt anyone. Then you're going to talk to me until you're all talked out."

Twenty-Six

IT HAD BEEN impulse and unplanned, at least that's what I told myself, that led to me becoming pregnant that September. Although I sensed that my conversation with Vanessa, which left me feeling confident and stopped me from telling Pax what had been on my mind, had played a hand in my outcome. Regardless of the reason, I was pregnant, and I was euphoric. My world had once again righted itself. The mere thought that I was carrying our baby made the past fade away like snow on a warm, sunny day. Painful memories dulled and forgotten, the now became memorable, and our baby and Pax were the only two things on my mind.

This time, I took time off work to focus on the baby's well-being. I hated to hand my children over to a substitute teacher, but I did so without hesitation.

The days following fell into an easy, relaxing pattern. I spent my days reading or going for short walks. The neighborhood was beginning to turn from green into the vibrant rusts and coppers of fall, and a cool air replaced the warmth of summer. Change, I thought, was a welcome constant in our lives.

I spent time catching up with friends, and Vanessa came by as often as she could, although most of her time was taken up with Tom, who was seemingly helping her heal the deep wounds inflicted by Jameson all those years ago. Vanessa had entered a new phase of her life, one that filled her with a happiness she hadn't known was possible, and I was thrilled for her and grateful to Tom. She was finally getting on with her life and allowing the love of a man into her life.

When the days got colder and shorter, I spent less time outside, opting for the warmth of my solarium. As the doctor ordered, I made sure to exercise with a daily swim.

All was perfect with my world and my baby.

PAX WALKED INTO THE SOLARIUM, HIS hair still wet and clinging to his skin. The fresh scent of soap and man all around him, and I breathed it in. We'd been married under three years, but he could still send my heart fluttering in the same way he had that first night we met. If, as Vanessa said, he didn't know how to live without me, I wouldn't know how I would cope without him. The notion that I'd thought of telling him he should leave me and find comfort in the arms of another woman seemed ludicrous to me now. I was eternally grateful to Vanessa for setting me straight when my mind had been a muddled mess.

Many were the nights when I still counted the minutes to his arrival home from work, looking forward to our dinners and chats. My days filled with little excitement, I listened intently as Pax told me about his. To most, our life seemed simple, uneventful, but to me it was tremendously satisfying. Spending time with Pax always felt fulfilling and indescribably romantic.

I had everything I wanted, everything I needed.

With his customary late-evening glass of wine in hand, he sat next to me. "You look nice and relaxed."

"Too relaxed." I set my book aside.

"I know you're bored, and you miss your school children and the interaction with your friends at work, but rest and relaxation is what the doctor ordered, and that's exactly what you're going to get." Pax brushed his lips against mine, and I tasted the sweetness of red on them.

"Agreed, but I am going crazy. Relaxation is overrated." I stretched my legs and set my feet on his lap.

"How about I treat you to dinner at The Bistro tomorrow night? We can take a short walk on the boardwalk afterwards," Pax said casually, and when I nodded excitedly, his lips curved into a smile. "I thought that would do it. I'll have Nora make the reservations."

"I'll do it. It'll give me something to do."

"What were you up to today?" He traced his thumb down the middle of my foot to my toes and repeated the motion.

"My mother and Caterina took me shopping."

"I hope you didn't spend all day on your feet." Stray beads of water from his hair had made their way down to his T-shirt, and his neck and shoulders were damp. I thought there was nothing sexier.

"I didn't. We shopped just long enough to fill my daily exercise requirement."

"I'm glad to hear." He took and indulgent sip then, began working on my other foot.

"I finished our Christmas shopping, although it didn't really feel Christmassy."

"I know it's only November, but I don't want you traipsing through the stores during those stressful shopping weeks." Pax ran the heel of his hand against the soles of my feet as I liked, making me shiver in pleasure.

"Anyway, we made plans for Will's first Christmas, and I'm really looking forward to it. He's going to love it."

Pax let out a booming laugh. "Sweets, he's only going to be nine months old. I doubt he's going to remember any of it when he gets older."

"Good experiences are an important part of child's development. Experiences, good or bad, have an impact throughout our entire life."

Knowing better than to argue with me, Pax mumbled, "Uh-huh," as he reached for his wine.

"Besides, after the scare we had those few weeks Will spent in the hospital, I want to make his first Christmas a grand one for him. I've been baking all sorts of traditional Christmas cookies for him to munch on." When Pax's brows arched, I laughed. "Well, mostly for us to munch on."

Pax took the last of his wine in one swallow. "I need a refill. Would you like more cranberry juice?" When I nodded, he got to his feet. "I'm assuming Michael's going to be at your mother's yearly Christmas lunch?" Pax called out from the kitchen.

"I'm guessing he will be." My eyes drifted to the horizon, where a half-moon floated and made trees stand in silhouette against a velvet black sky.

"That's too bad. Have your mother or sister said anything more about his whereabouts the night she went into labor?" Pax handed me the glass of juice.

"They never did, and after the couple of times I alluded to it and got the brush off, I thought it best to steer away from the topic. The whole thing leaves me feeling guilty. I mean, I want to tell her what we…I suspect." I immediately corrected myself when I got a raised brow.

"What's wrong?" Pax asked when I suddenly went quiet.

"It feels wrong not telling Caterina. I've felt so conflicted ever since we first spoke about it. I mean, to suspect your sister's husband of sleeping around and not be able to tell her. Whether we get along or not, she's my sister."

"I know it's a horrible position to be in, but you have no proof, sweets."

"I have a gut feeling and it's telling me that that's exactly what he's doing." I watched Pax methodically run his fingers up and down the stem of his glass.

"Instinct is not proof. Think about it. You could potentially destroy a marriage with allegations. Besides, you have more important issues to think about right now." He set his hand on my tummy, pressing it against the child that was already beautiful and real to us. "You and this baby are what are important to me. I want you to avoid stress and to stay rested and relaxed. Leave your sister to deal with her husband." His eyes pressed for my acknowledgement.

"All right, I will."

"Why don't you invite Vanessa and this Danny friend of hers to join us for dinner tomorrow night?"

"It's Tom right now."

Pax's eyes registered surprise. "She's back with Tom? I can't keep up with that woman."

"Tom works with you. Do you not know anything about the man?" "Do you not know anything about the man?" He teasingly mimicked me. "I know everything there is to know about his work life. I don't need to know anything about his personal life. Anyway, he is a glutton for punishment, isn't he?"

I nodded with a smile. "He is, but I sense this time it's getting serious between them. And I'm so happy for her, for them. It's a long time coming, but she's finally letting someone into her heart, into her life, and I'm so glad it's Tom. No one will love her more than he will. She deserves to be happy. Maybe tomorrow night you can get the scoop from his perspective."

"That's not going to happen." Pax made a face that made me laugh aloud.

"Sorry, I lost my head there for a moment. No personal talk around you."

He squeezed my hand. "What do you say to the three of us going up to bed?"

"Mommy and baby say yes please," my voice sang in response.

IN THE BEDROOM, AS I TOOK my clothes off, the familiar wave of despair washed over me as I looked down at my blood-stained panties.

Twenty-Seven

THE WORDS KEPT coming at me like sharp, jagged daggers after Dr. Baxter's left the office. All indication is that you will never be able to carry a baby to term, Natalia.

"Are you okay, sweets?" Pax asked quietly as he took my hand.

I never spoke. If I did, I'd break down.

Pax opened the door and poked his head out. In seconds, Dr. Baxter's secretary walked in with a glass of water. "Here you go, Mrs. Reed." The pity in her eyes was inescapable.

Was this the way it would always be?

The humiliation on top of the hurt was more than I could stand. "I don't want any water."

"Drink some," Pax said taking the glass and setting it in my hands when she'd left us.

I did. It did nothing to ease the nausea grinding in my stomach.

All indication is that you will never be able to carry a baby to term, Natalia. They came at me again. This time the words cut cleanly to the bone, at my self-worth, at my feminine sensibility, to my heart and soul. They scarred and broke me. I'd never be able to have the child I had always wanted. I would never be a mother. I would never make Pax a father. I would never make us a family.

I was not a woman.

From the window of Dr. Baxter's office, I watched gloomy gray clouds roll in to obscure the late morning sun, and I thought how apt.

Pax simply held me. His shoulder cushioning my head, for a long while, we fell into an uneasy silence, our burdened thoughts remaining our own.

When I finally said, "We need to get another opinion," the words came out in half a sob.

"Sweets, Dr. Baxter is the top specialist in the country." His voice was soft.

The sky was now black, and a moisture thick air warned of the incoming rain. Seconds later, a white bolt exploded somewhere in the distance, and lanced the sky.

I wanted to cry, but my anger took over. "I don't care if he's God. I want another opinion."

"But…"

"I refused to accept his findings. There has to be something someone can do. There has to be."

There was surprise and despair in his eyes. I know that what he wanted was this door closed and the key thrown away—for both our sakes. "You've put yourself through enough already."

I looked him in the eyes. "You mean you've put yourself through enough."

"That's not at all what I meant."

I bolted to my feet, and began to pace the room with a furious energy. "Well, I'm not giving up. With or without you I will go from doctor to doctor. There has to be a doctor out there who can help me. Who will understand what it is to be told, as a woman, you can't bear a child. A simple, natural function women perform day in and day out." I needed Pax, someone, anyone to understand that this was about wanting a baby so much that I would do anything, undergo any emotional or physical pain necessary.

Pax rose, and calmly walked over to the window where I stood. "With me."

"What?"

"You said, 'with or without you.' And I'm saying that it'll be with me." He tucked a strand of hair behind my ears. "Are you okay with that?"

"I am." My face settle against his chest I breathed him in as I cried my silent tears.

A booming thunder rolled in, and the slashing rain came down in sheets beating hard against the window. Within seconds, the world outside was drenched. The curtain of rain washing down the windows felt like my shattered dreams.

"There has to be something someone can do," I said under my breath, but in my heart, I knew better. I knew there was nothing anyone could do. I was infertile. Remaining childless was my destiny. I stared down at the water in my glass. "I'm sorry, Pax."

"What could you possibly need to apologize for?"

"I'm the one who can't make us a family. It's me who will never be able to give you the family you want. I'm barren, Pax," I said cringing at the repulsive sounding word, which not only breaks you, but deprives you of your femininity, your role as a woman.

For a few seconds, the sky flashed white as lightning struck and the ensuing thunder boomed as loud as detonating cannons.

"Don't you see, Pax? This doesn't end here and now. This will be with me for the rest of my life. I will carry this grief for the rest of my life. I'll never be able to get away from it, and neither will you. There will be constant reminders all around us—always. Friends, family, and even strangers will always be having children, celebrating their children. There will always be the sound of children around us. Their infectious laughter piercing our ears will always bring us back to this moment. For God sakes, I'm a schoolteacher surrounded by children. All that will remind us, me, again and again that I couldn't give you children."

"You're hurting right now." His hand closed over mine, and I tore it away.

"The hopelessness and helplessness and guilt will break me. I'll hate myself, I'll make you hate me, and we'll end up hating each other. I'll cry it off, and you may too, but in the end, I alone bear the responsibility of failing you. I will always know that I, me, failed to make you the family you wanted, and I can't bear the guilt of knowing that."

As I looked deep into his eyes, I watched them film over, and my guilt for causing him to feel this way made my heart hammer in my chest. As Pax opened his mouth to say something, I waved a hand to silence him.

"I don't want to drag you down into my misery, because I'm…barren." There was that vile word again leaving a bitter taste in my mouth. I took a sip of water to wash it away. "Time does heal, but it will take years for me to come to terms with it. I don't want to deprive you of the family you've always wanted, Pax. I love you too much to take that from you." It was cold comfort, but I felt better for having put my feelings into the words he needed to hear.

"You are my family."

There was so much emotion in his words, my throat closed in on me. "But, Pax…"

"I know this has been difficult for you, and I've been useless to you, but I'm a man. You have to understand we're not equipped to deal with situations like these." There was ache in his voice, grief in his eyes.

"No, you've been perfect. Patient and caring and there for me every step of the way, it's why you deserve better than me, Pax."

"Sweets?" He pinched my chin, to tilt my face up to his, and I allowed myself to absorb the feel of his touch. The shock of realization that it was something I may never feel again made me miserable, but I willed my gaze steady, and my eyes to remain dry.

"The best moments in my life have come from being with you. I will never find a better woman than you. You've put yourself through so much for us. I'm so grateful to you for giving so much of yourself. I never want to hear you apologizing again nor do I want you thinking that we'll never be a family, because we already are a complete family. I've told you that no matter what life brings, we, you and me, will deal with it and I meant every word. You'll have to get used to the fact that you're stuck with me, because I'm not going anywhere. You mean everything to me. You're the most important person in my life. I love you. As long as there's a breath in my body, I will always love you."

The sincerity in his tone, the way he looked at me, made me feel complete, and I felt the emotions for Pax rolling in me like powerful ocean waves. "I couldn't imagine riding this journey through life with anyone else but you."

I fell into the warmth of his protective arms. My face buried in his chest, for a long while, he held me close, the rise and fall of his chest against my ear soothed as I cried my silent tears.

"I will always be by your side, sweets," he whispered into my hair. "It's the two of us against anything that comes our way."

The words arrowed straight into my heart, and I didn't know it then, but they would echo in me for the rest of my life.

Twenty-Eight

THE FOLLOWING MONTHS saw me suffer another miscarriage, undergo more invasive tests, meet with more specialists, all to result in more disappointment, more heartache, and pain. Hopes shattered, the glow of motherhood was extinguished forever.

I didn't know how difficult it would be to let go of something I never had.

By the time Christmas came around, I wanted no part of it. I wanted to be left alone. I wanted to hide in a faraway place where doctors, needles, hospitals, and recovery rooms didn't exist. But for Will's benefit, who at almost two years old, the excitement of Christmas, presents, a flashing tree, decorations, and his loving family around him was what he needed, I put on the appropriate display of holiday cheer.

"Merry Christmas, Mom," I said, in the most upbeat tone I could muster when she opened the door looking festive in the red Versace silk dress with a green belt.

"Merry Christmas. Come on in out of the cold." My mother stepped aside and waved Pax and me in.

Her eyes immediately homed in on the dark circles and tired look on my face, and to my surprise, no criticism followed. Instead, she took me in for an unexpected embrace.

"How are you, dear?" she asked, studying me with a watchful eye.

"Natalia's doing fine, Rose," Pax answered on my behalf knowing that if I answered the conversation would slip into a probe of my emotional well-being, which I wasn't inclined to deal with then.

My mother was about to say something when a squealing Will toddled out into the foyer with a stoic Caterina trailing. He wore a red overall with a green and white striped shirt, and moccasins at his feet. His hair, lightened since birth, was now a honey blonde, and his eyes were inquisitive and sky blue. He looked adorable and every bit the image of Michael.

"Merry Christmas," Caterina said, then scooped Will into her arms and held him far enough to avoid little fingers from leaving prints on her dress.

"Sorry, Mom, I guess I should have worn something other than jeans and a sweater," I said eyeing Caterina, who looked stylishly chic in the Chanel suit that spoke of elegance and suited the willowy figure she'd reclaimed weeks after Will's birth. Her hair, luxuriously blonde and shiny spilled around her face and down her back. At her ears and neck diamonds the size of grapes sparkled.

My mother waved a dismissive hand. "Nonsense, you must wear what makes you feel most comfortable." Her comment sent the room into a momentary stunned silence.

"Do you like them?" Caterina pushed the curling spill of hair back to run a perfectly manicured finger to her ear lobe. "It's Michael's Christmas present. Aren't they yummy? They're three carats, princess diamond studs."

"They're beautiful, Cat," I said.

Focused on her image in the hall mirror, Caterina turned right and left so the stone caught the light. "They are, aren't they? Did I mention they're three carats?"

"You did." I reached for Will when Caterina, engrossed in herself, ignored his appeals for her attention.

Pax stepped in to take Will from Caterina's arms. "I'll take him. Let's get you settled on the couch, sweets, and I'll set this happy boy on your lap." Pax leaned in closer when Will's tiny fingers reached out to caress Pax's cheek, and when Pax stuck his tongue out at him, Will broke out in hysterical laughter. The sight tugged at my heart, but I managed to keep a smile in place.

The moment we stepped into the living room, Will's eyes rounded and he began to squeal with delight, pudgy hands waving frantically.

My mother had transformed the living room into the Christmas card of my youth. Logs snapped and sizzled in the fireplace, its mantel adorned with seven hanging stockings—one for each one of us. Red and white poinsettias sat on tables throughout the room. The sweet smell of pine from the ten-foot Balsam twinkling under dozens of colorful lights and adorned with the expertly placed antique ornaments scented the room and ruled the large bay window. Beneath it, there were presents, loads of them wrapped and bowed. Beyond the tree, an orange moon cast a warm glow as snowflakes drifted in a cold wind and shrouded the city in white.

The scene brought back so many wonderful memories of my childhood, and I felt my heart clench at the thought that I'd never be able to make my own memories with my child.

"This young man is pretty heavy." Pax set Will down on my lap with such tenderness and care that left both my mother and Caterina watching on with what I thought was appreciation on my mother's part and envy from Caterina. "You sure you're all right with him, sweets?"

"I am, because you are the loveliest baby," I said raising Will's hand to my mouth and kissing his palm. Will's response was an enthusiastic squeal and just then I felt Pax's gaze on me. When I looked over to him, I could see the flash of sadness in his eyes. Whether for himself or for me I wasn't sure; regardless, it cut deep into my heart and I uncomfortably shifted in my seat.

Mistaking my movement for discomfort my mother was quick to ask, "Are you sure you're all right with him, dear? Will is a bit of a chunky boy and you shouldn't be lifting anything heavy."

"Oh, that's right. You had surgery, exploratory or something of the sort, didn't you?" Caterina said her tone detached and cold.

"It's been a few months now." I kept my eyes focused on Will.

"Did they finally figure out why you've had so many miscarriages? It's your fourth, isn't it?" Caterina asked.

I blinked the tears back and did my best to remain composed when the familiar sense of guilt and inadequacy washed over me.

"That's enough, Caterina." An audible anger edged my mother's voice.

To my surprise—and hers—Caterina skirted over my mother's scorn. "Do they know why it's happening? Why it is that you keep on having all these miscarriages?"

"No." I watched Caterina casually pour herself a brandy at the bar, and I wondered what had turned my sister into this cold, heartless woman I no longer recognized.

"It's weird how things work out. I get pregnant with Will without really wanting to." When her comment didn't get the reaction she hoped for, she added, "I didn't want Will. I never wanted to have any children, not with Michael, anyway."

The room simultaneously turned a shocked gaze toward Caterina.

Thinking it wise to remove Pax from the conversation, my mother said, "Pax, Rob and Michael are in the wine cellar selecting the wines for our Christmas dinner." Once Pax stepped out of the room, flushed with rage my mother turned to Caterina. "That's the most cold-hearted thing I have yet heard you say. Not to mention an insensitive comment to make in front of your sister."

Sinking herself in the wingback across from me, Caterina crossed long, toned legs. "Well, it's the truth, Mother. I had Will simply as a means of survival. I had to have him to ensure an heir to the precious Stanton fortune and secure my marriage to Michael or at the least a connection to him for life."

Stunned by her candid remarks, Mom and I gaped at her. It was that dazed look that came with shock, and, open-mouthed, we both stared at Caterina for a long while before my mother broke the silence.

"Really, Caterina, why would you even feel the need to openly make such a statement?"

Caterina laughed despairingly, her eyes clouded with cynicism. "Oh, Mother, please don't act so sanctimonious. You of all people should understand. You're the one who wanted this marriage, and when you figured out that Natalia would never agree to marry Michael, you steered him in my direction. Bringing the Stanton name into the family fold was a dream of yours since the day Daddy partnered with Blake. Wasn't it, Mother?"

My mother pressed a hand to her temple, as if willing to stop the conversation. "It certainly was not. God, Caterina, the things that come out of your mouth sometimes," she said getting to her feet and making a quick dash for the bar. Mom drained her first pour of brandy in one gulp and immediately topped her glass with three more fingers.

Caterina turned toward my mother. "I'm not saying I didn't want Michael. I'm just saying you sped things along because Michael was the apple of your eye. But Mother, I have news for you. Michael never wanted me, and as for loving me…" Caterina let out a scathing snort. "Well, let's just say that Michael only loves Michael. The universe revolves around the magnificent Michael Stanton. I found that out the hard way." Caterina turned green eyes on me. "You are so lucky you followed your heart, Natalia, and didn't listen to her. If you had you would be with some rich, pompous tool, with a pretentious last name, who'd lavish you with nothing but money." She rolled scathing eyes toward my mother.

"But I guess it's the price one pays to indulge in the lifestyle men like Michael brings with them. Life is all about tit-for-tat. Nothing comes without a price. Unfortunately, once you get accustomed to that cushy lifestyle, it's hard to give it up. So, at this point, I'm willing to do anything to maintain it, even if it meant having a baby I didn't want. I figured I'd give him the heir that he and his parents so desperately wanted, which is really the only reason he married me, and in the process, I'd guarantee myself this wonderful, luxurious lifestyle I've become so attached to. That little sweetheart—" her heavily lined eyes drifted over to Will "—is going to ensure Mommy's happiness."

I recoiled at the callousness in her tone. "Jesus, Cat."

"Really, Caterina, I didn't think I'd raised a child of mine to be so…self-serving." My mother's steely eyes stared Caterina down, while my terribly saddened gaze rested on the sleeping child in my arms.

When I looked up, I saw my mother's hands trembling as she again topped up her glass and took a gulp.

"It's not self-serving, Mother. It's survival, because Michael has roving eyes, and I can't trust him as far as I can throw him." At the look of shock on my mother's face, Caterina continued. "Yes, Mother, the man you've set up on this pedestal of perfectionism is a philanderer, a womanizer who doesn't think twice about screwing any woman who will let him. You know that perfect relationship you boast to your friends about? It's not mine and Michael's, it's Natalia and Pax's. That holier-than-thou son-in-law who can do no wrong in your eyes doesn't exist in Michael."

When Caterina saw my mother's breath hitch, she rolled frosted eyes. "And don't play the pious card on me, Mother. I learned everything I know from you."

My mother's hand closed over her chest, and her expression was a mixture of anger and disappointment. "Why are you saying such horrible things, Caterina?"

"Because, Mother, someone should point out what you can't see." Caterina then turned her gaze to me. "Pax loves you, Natalia, and he only wants you. You can see it in his eyes, in the tender way he touches you, in the loving way he speaks to you. You have a hold on him most of us can only dream of. You will never have to ask yourself if you're enough for him, if he needs you, because you will always be and he will always need you. You will never know what it's like not to trust your husband or wonder whether he will be coming home that night, and if he does come home, whose bed he was in before slipping into yours out of a sense of contractual obligation, because that's what marriage becomes at that point. Pax's eyes will never wander to any other woman as Michael's and…Daddy's have. Isn't that right, Mom?"

My mother shot Caterina a look that could have frozen fire. "Don't bring your father into this, Caterina."

"Why not, Mom? Didn't you say, 'One needs to know the truth so one can make informed decisions'? Yes, you heard right, Natalia. Daddy has gone astray on at least one occasion that Mother's told me about." Caterina's words roused the intended shock in me. "So, you really didn't know. I guess I was privy to Mother's secrets because she knew Michael, like Daddy, needed to be reined in."

I stepped into the conversation in a hushed voice as a sleeping Will shifted in my arms. "What are you talking about?"

"Daddy dipped his company pen into one of his employees." Caterina's callous eyes stared at me over the rim of her glass.

"Don't be so crude, Caterina. It's not becoming." My mother refilled her drink—again. She was already one quarter into the brandy bottle.

The thought of my father cheating on my mother, and with someone I almost certainly knew, was like a grenade to my system. "Who? When? Not Daddy?"

"Yes, Daddy. Doesn't really matter. It was a long time ago, and Mother managed to put a stop to it after a few months. Didn't you, Mom?" Caterina glared directly into my mother's distressed eyes, now deepened in color.

"Stop it now, Caterina," my mother demanded.

Caterina dismissed the plea and went on. "Like Mother, I did what I thought was necessary to keep Michael coming back to me. I did everything he wanted, but you and I know that when you marry a philanderer, which Michael undoubtedly is, no effort you put into a marriage is going to keep him from seeking comfort in the arms of another. But that little bundle will certainly ensure he keeps coming back to me." Caterina's voice was steel.

Looking down at the innocent child in my arms, who, by his mother's admission, was being used as a pawn, the angered pulsed inside my chest. I'd never felt more resentful of my sister than I did at that moment.

"Jesus, Cat, how could you?"

"It's easy for you to judge, Natalia, when you have a man like Pax. A man who will never give you reason to doubt his love for you. He loves you, as I've never seen a man love a woman. Your difficulties over the past couple of years have only brought him closer to you. And I can guarantee you that, regardless of what the outcome of your issue is, he will always be by your side. A man and a love like Pax's are hard to find. I really do envy you, Natalia." From the expression on Caterina's face, I could see she was taken aback by her own admission. "It's not easy living with someone who has betrayed your trust again and again. It's draining and tiring." A hush weighed in the room until Caterina huffed out a breath.

"Well, I don't know about you, but I'm starving," she said, as my mother and I, in a state of shock, digested the past twenty-five minutes.

Twenty-Nine

DINNER WAS A difficult and awkward experience.

Caterina remained silent throughout the entire meal, moving food—which my mother had likely spent days planning—around on her plate. My mother was unusually quiet herself, spending most of her time darting hardened looks at Michael. Michael and Pax, who sat across from one another, didn't bother to hide their mutual disdain. I remained quiet, partly because my seething anger for Caterina added an additional layer of emotion to my already fragile state, and I didn't trust myself not to burst into tears or launch into a scathing argument with my sister. Luckily for everyone, my father was his jovial self and managed to carry on a one-sided conversation that gave the meal a semblance of holiday cheer.

After dinner, on my mother's suggestion, everyone reluctantly moved into the living room for coffee and dessert. Caterina, however, made a detour up the stairs, and I followed her, stopping in to check on a sleeping Will when she walked right past his room.

"Everything looks the same," I said, walking into Caterina's old bedroom and as I took a closer look, I realized the room looked lived-in.

Unlike my room, where closets were empty and the dresser displayed only pictures of my youth, there were shoes and clothes in the closet, and bottles of perfume, make-up and several night creams sat on the dressing table. I didn't venture to ask why they were there since she already looked annoyed by my mere presence.

"What do you want, Natalia?" Caterina's mouth tightened into a grim line.

"I wanted to get away for a bit."

"Well, that's exactly why I came upstairs. So, if you don't mind, close the door on your way out," she said laying down on her bed. A halo of blonde fanned around her making her look angelic.

"You look pale, Cat."

"I'm just tired."

I instinctively sensed there was much more than fatigue afflicting her. When the silence lengthened, I said, "I'm sorry about Michael."

"Not half as sorry as I am." Bitterness edged her words. "He's such an asshole. The worst part is that deep down I sensed he was like this all along and I still chose to marry him. I mean, you don't date someone for months and not pick up on their flaws. But he was such a good catch. He had everything a woman wants in a man: a prestigious name, the best education, financial stability, and for Mom's sake, he came from a reputable family." She sighed, closing her eyes briefly.

I wanted to point out that that wasn't what every woman looked for in a man, but I thought better of it and remained silent.

"On reflection, I think I conveniently dismissed his imperfections, hoping that the benefits would more than make up for his shortcomings."

"Do you love him, Cat?" She hadn't once made mention of the word.

Her gaze focused on some distant point, she thought about the question. "When Michael and I first came together, I couldn't stand him. I thought he was pompous, self-centered, with an air of entitlement, but Mom was so insistent on him becoming my husband that I didn't want to let her down, so I stuck it out with him. And I think in time, she steered me to see him in a different light. You know she's always seen him as this perfect, can-do-no-wrong type of man, so I came to see him that way too. After we got married..." Her words trailed off, and I could see her reflecting on long-buried memories. "Things were really great. For the first two years of our marriage, he was attentive, caring, loving, and I grew to love him more than I imagined possible. It was a time when I believed we had a solid future. His touch made my insides quiver like a bowl of Jell-O, and he sent my heart racing every time he was near me."

She absently smiled before her eyes went turbulent. "And overnight it all changed. I don't know if I triggered it or whether he became bored with me, with our marriage. With us." A wistful expression took over her face.

"You know, I did exactly what he wanted, how he wanted it. Michael can be a ...controlling man. I mean, I almost lost Will because he didn't like me gaining weight. But even after all the sacrifices I made, our marriage took a complete one-hundred-and-eighty-degree turn. Six years into our blessed union, he's become distant, moody, and it's been months since he's...touched me."

In the awkward silence, I could see the regret, anger, and fatigue in her eyes. The river of pain. I wanted to reach out a hand to her as an unspoken sign of support, but I didn't. Cold eyes told me she'd discount the gesture.

"I'm sorry, Cat."

"So to answer your question, no, I don't love him. Not anymore. How can I invest emotion in such an egotistical person? Besides, his long absences and ongoing affairs tell me he doesn't want to revive our marriage or have anything to do with it."

"What makes you think he's having an affair?"

"Affairs," she corrected stressing the S. "A wife knows. He's 'working'—" she air-quoted the word "—excessively long hours, and he spends a lot of time traveling for the company. That's what he claims, but I know better."

I could hear the sadness and loneliness in her voice. For a moment, I was too stunned to speak.

"Have you talked to Daddy? Asked him about possibly taking some responsibilities from Michael so he could spend more time at home?"

She nodded. "I alluded to it, and Daddy told me that Pax has taken over most of Michael's responsibilities and he now barely puts in a twenty-hour week. But Daddy can only attest to the work Michael does for Stanton and Rossi, not the work he does for many of his father's other businesses as he claimed to do when I confronted him."

"What about talking to Blake or Diana?"

"I wouldn't dare talk to them. When our marriage started going downhill, I decided that his money was going to fill the void in our marriage, and I started to spend his money indiscriminately. I lavished myself with designer clothes, shoes, handbags, jewelry. I traveled on the Stanton private jet with friends to Paris, Rome, London, Fiji, Bora

Bora. I was living it up, and Michael didn't seem to mind in the least. It was in his best interest that I kept busy. With me out of his hair, it meant fewer arguments and more time to himself—to do as he wanted. But, as with everything in life, all good things must come to an end, and my spending spree was brought to an abrupt halt by Diana. She stepped in to rein me in, or, as she referred to it, 'control the abuse of their money.' If I say anything to them, they'll think it's the rantings of a nagging, spoiled wife whose hand is no longer allowed in the Stanton cookie jar. Mother knows nothing about all this. It wouldn't make any difference anyway. She's blinded by them."

For the first time, I understood Caterina, and I felt shame well up in my chest at not being a better older sister. As if reading my mind, she said, "Don't feel bad, Natalia. I haven't been a good sister to you."

"How could you be when I haven't told you much about anything?"

"You don't, but Mom tells me everything. I know you've just found out you'll never be able to have children, and I'm very sorry about that. I know how much you love children and wanted one of your own." Hearing the words when Caterina spoke them made me feel like the incomplete woman that I sensed everyone now saw me as, and I bit the tears back. "One positive in your life, Natalia, is Pax. Even after your life-changing event, Pax is standing by your side. The man absolutely adores you. I'll never know what that feels like."

I thought then of Pax's words before doctor gave us the devastating news. *Regardless of what Dr. Baxter's findings are, sweets, I want you to know that I love you and I always will.*

"I don't have the luxury of having a loving man by my side, nor am I as strong as you. I need to focus on me and me alone." She held my gaze, and I nodded in understanding as she expected me to. "So you see, Natalia, you and Mom can judge me all you want, but what I'm doing is a matter of survival. I've accepted the fact that I can't change Michael and that I'll never have the enviable type of relationship you and Pax have. I don't even feel anymore, Natalia. When I try, it hurts too much. It's best not to try at all, and I focus on Michael's money. It's the only thing I have left, and I'm sure as hell not going to let him take that from me, least of all let his whores at it. It's unfortunate that I'm using Will as a pawn, but I will do anything and everything to keep his money, the thing he cherishes above all else, and which I've come to appreciate, tied to me."

I knew we were at a crossroads then, because I couldn't agree with her tactics. "Couldn't you find another way?"

"Says you, with the perfect husband, the house you can call a home, the rewarding career." The words were said with an edge of bitterness. She rose from the bed and sat at the dresser, stared at herself in the mirror as if searching for the woman she used to be. "All I have now is loads and loads of money."

"Cat, you have Will." Lost eyes met mine in the mirror. "I see so much of Michael in Will, and God help me, but there are times when…" Her hands absently balled into fists. "I've clung to a despairing grief that was destroying my soul, but I soon realized that clinging to anger was less agonizing than clinging to grief and far more productive when it came to vengeful designs. That was when I decided to have Will." Caterina dabbed Chanel behind her ears and ran a brush through her hair. "I figured that if Michael was going to continue with his philandering, completely disregard our marriage and disrespect me, his money was going to fill the void. Will secures my association to the Stanton name and their fortune."

I found myself thinking that not once had she referred to Will as her son, and I felt immensely sad for that child.

"You don't know for certain that Michael is…?"

Caterina finished for me. "Screwing around on me?" When I nodded, she reached into her dresser drawer and retrieved a thick manila envelope. "I had a private investigator follow him a few months back," she explained as I began to thumb through the dozens of photographs. "Even Mom hasn't seen those. As you can see, there's a selection of women in the pictures, which, believe it or not, doesn't really bother me. The fleeting women in his life tell me he has no emotional attachment to them. But there's one who off and on slides in and out of his life. She has for the past three years, which drives me to believe that she's more than a good screw." Her voice was so mild in contrast to the hardened expression on her face.

"Do you know who she is?" I asked.

She shook her head "This is a photograph of her. It was taken from too far away to depict anything but a grainy silhouette. Yet every time I look at it, I can't help but feel as I know who she is."

When she handed me the photograph, my stomach flipped and eyes unintentionally widened.

"You know her. You know who she is."

"I can't be certain. It looks like her."

"Who is she? Who's the shameless, fucking slut who's been spreading her legs for him and threatening my welfare?"

Not once did she give thought to Will's welfare or her marriage. It was all about her own personal wellbeing. I didn't know this woman.

"Who is she?" she prodded.

"You've met her," I said.

"When? I can't place her."

"She's Pax's assistant. She was sitting next to Michael at Pax's Christmas party last year."

"Jesus fucking Christ! Are you talking about that homely looking woman?" She glared at me skeptically. "No way. It can't be her. She's not Michael's type."

"Her name is Nora Wells. And I don't believe Michael's emotionally invested in her. My guess is his…interest in her is solely to get information."

"What are you talking about?"

"Michael has almost zero influence or responsibility in Stanton and Rossi or any of Blake's businesses." I went on to explain when shock filled her face. "Pax has taken over all of Michael's company responsibilities and I'm guessing he is likely exploiting Nora to get inside information on the projects Pax is working on for Daddy and Blake. To sabotage them in order to tarnish Pax and cause him to lose the Stanton and Rossi account."

"No I…I didn't know. I…uh, I can't believe any of this," she stammered. "He's sleeping with this sad excuse of a woman, when he's got me for vengeance? I…I can't…wrap my head around any of this. You know what she looks like. Why would he when he's got this?" She skimmed hands up and down herself, and as sorry as I felt for her, I thought how perfectly paired she, and Michael were.

Will's cries pierced our conversation and she let out an annoyed sigh.

"I'll look after him," I said, needing the distraction.

"Okay. Boy, am I glad I decided to have Will. Even if Blake and Diana disown their son, I know for a fact they will never disown their only grandson, or me. Will is mine and I will make sure they know it."

She was the mirror image of Michael, and she would never see that. "I'll tell Pax about Nora," I said and when she looked up the sadness in her eyes tugged at me. We all had our crosses to bear, but a life without love, which I believed—by her own choosing—she was destined to live, made the journey a difficult one. "And I'm sorry, Cat. You don't deserve this."

She pursed her lips in a half smile.

Stopping in the doorway, I took one last look at my sister. Her shoulders erect, her head held high, she turned to freshen her make-up.

I'd never felt sadder for her than I did then.

IT WAS NEARING EIGHT WHEN PAX and I left my parents' house. A chilly curtain of thick snow fell, camouflaging iced roads under a film of white and leaving Pax to maneuver his way down slick roads.

"That was a scary drive," Pax said as he pulled the car into our garage.

"Not half as scary as this whole day has been. I have a lot to tell you. Some you're not going to like."

"That sounds ominous. Why don't I get the fireplace going while you open a bottle of wine? Then we can talk and eventually get to those presents under the tree," he said with a wicked wiggle of eyebrows that made me laugh.

"That sounds like a perfect idea." I kissed him, filling myself of the taste of him.

"What was that for?"

"Have I told you what a wonderful husband you are and how much I love you?"

"Once or twice before."

"Then I don't say it often enough, and my new year's resolution is to say it more."

"All right, and I'm going to hold you to that, but for now we need to get inside the house. It's freezing out here."

As soon as Pax shut the front door behind us, the telephone sounded.

"Hi, Tom. Merry Christmas," Pax's voice sang out. "Is she all right? Is...everything okay?" When his eyes widened, a jolt of fear sprang hot to my throat. "We'll be there as soon as we can."

"What's wrong?"

Uneasy eyes rose to meet mine. "It's Vanessa. She's been in a serious car accident."

Thirty

FOUR HOURS AFTER my last conversation with Dr. Steward, she walked into the waiting room. The hazel eyes looked as rested as I felt after my short nap forced on me by Pax.

I bolted to my feet. "Do you have any news on Vanessa? Please doctor, I can't continue to sit around not knowing."

"I do. I have the test results I was waiting for. Please have a seat." Dr. Steward gestured us down as she herself sank into a chair. "I want to assure you that my team and I are doing everything we can for Vanessa. She's getting the best care in the country, and we're doing everything to decrease the intracranial pressure, which is now our major concern, as—" She stopped long enough to read her buzzing pager before continuing. "As is the well-being of the baby."

There was a stunned silence. The sound of total disbelief.

"A baby? What are you talking about?" I said.

Dr. Steward flickered her attention from that Goddamn pager to us. "Her hCG levels were high, and I thought it prudent to requisition a pregnancy test. It was one of the results I was waiting on. Vanessa is nine weeks pregnant."

I froze, paralyzed with a new layer of shock. Sitting there like a statue, the blood pounding in my ears created a buzzing sound that deafened me. I was certain I'd heard wrongly. A baby? Vanessa pregnant? This had to be a mistake—a monumental one. When the heat of shock had snaked through my system, I opened my mouth to ask the hundreds of questions flashing in my mind, but my mouth was so dry and my tongue so thick, that nothing came out.

"The baby is fine?" Tom said.

The crushing weight on my chest made it so I couldn't breathe. Huffing for air, the room began to spin and I began to feel faint.

"Lower your head and place it between your knees," Dr. Steward watched to make sure I did it right. "You'll feel better in a moment," she said then, proceeded to answer Tom. "Yes, the baby is perfectly fine, and we're going to do everything in our power to ensure Vanessa remains in stable condition for her and her baby's sake."

Tom asked. "Will the baby affect Vanessa's well-being?"

"It's still too soon to tell, but the baby may put a strain on her body."

"What happens to the baby if Vanessa doesn't come out of her coma?" Pax visibly stricken, pointedly asked.

"Feeling better?" Dr. Steward asked, when my head came back up. When I nodded, she went on to answer Pax's question. "The unknowns are many in a case such as this one. There have been a handful of medically documented cases where women have been kept alive through artificial means until they delivered their babies. We certainly want to give the baby every chance of survival. If Vanessa remains comatose, we'll need to prolong pregnancy for as long as possible. We'd like to aim for thirty-two weeks, but if it becomes medically impossible, we'll aim for a delivery in the twenty-fourth week. A delivery earlier than that would not allow the baby to survive outside the womb. Even at twenty-four weeks, the baby is likely to require neonatal care for weeks." Her voice remained levelled as she laid out the scenarios.

Tom's eyes swam with grief as he quietly listened. "Please, doctor, do what you can for the baby's sake. This pregnancy is important to her."

Pax added. "Yes, please doctor. She'd want that."

Dr. Steward's unwavering eyes met Tom and Pax's. "We will. If you'll excuse me, I really need to get back." With a flourish, Dr. Steward got to her feet, and a moment later, she was gone.

RUBBING AT THE THROBBING PAIN BUILDING up at my temples, I sat there in a dreamlike trance. Vanessa was nine weeks pregnant and she'd never once mentioned it to me. She hadn't even hinted at it. My best friend, the person I confided in, the person I trusted more than my own sister and mother, the woman who knew my darkest secrets hadn't thought to tell me her monumental news. Being pregnant was titanic-size news in itself, but the fact that it was Vanessa the mother-to-be upped the ante by a factor of one trillion. Still, she thought best to keep it from me. Out of pity, I decided. It was the only reason I could think of why she wouldn't want to tell me. I'd become that infertile woman who couldn't create a life and who everyone now pitied, even my best friend.

I tried to swallow, but the bitter taste stuck in my throat.

"Sweets, why don't you sit down?" Pax's voice filled my head.

Emotions burning with temper had me lashing out. "I don't want to sit down," I said then, turned blazing eyes to Tom. "When did you find out about Vanessa's pregnancy?"

Tom met my eyes. "I only found out a few days ago, Natalia."

I raised disbelieving brows. "How could you just be finding this out now?"

"I swear to you, Natalia. I only found out about her pregnancy when she told me. I wouldn't have known otherwise. It's too early to visually detect." He looked to Pax for affirmation.

Nodding, Pax turned to me. "He's right, sweets."

"Pax wouldn't be able to tell, but you've been bedding her for the past few weeks. How could you not know?" My words tumbled out with an undeserving anger at Tom.

Pax hastily jumped in with, "Jesus, Natalia."

"It's all right, Pax." Tom hesitated for a moment, and set eyes on his hands studying them. "We haven't been…close in a while, Natalia. She told me she isn't in love me. That she's in love with another man." His eyes were filled with a genuine sadness, but I refused to see it and I gave in to temper and impulse.

"It's not your baby?" I waited for his response. Waited, and waited.

"No, it's not." Tom dragged a hand through dark hair.

I could hear the regret and disappointment in his tone, and still I plowed on with the question I knew would be painful for him. "Whose is it?"

Clouded eyes looked up at me. "I don't know. I know it's not mine."

Pax gave me a subtle headshake and mouthed a silent, "Sweets, stop."

The words shot a dose of reality into the moment. It wasn't Tom I was angry with. I was angry with myself for becoming that barren woman whom everyone, including my best friend, felt sorry for. "I'm sorry, Tom. I was out of line. I know you care for her," I said, but Tom didn't acknowledge my words, he simply continued to stare at his hands, as if lost in them. "I feel like I let her down. I've made it so she can't talk to me. I'm supposed to be her friend," I said in an attempt to justify my actions.

"Don't be so hard on yourself. Knowing Vanessa, she must have her reasons, benign as they are, for not telling you."

"Pax is right, Natalia. Vanessa does have her reasons, and it's not because, as you think, she can't talk to you about it, but because she doesn't want you to get your hopes up." Tom's voice was low and calm now.

"What do you mean, get my hopes up?"

An ensuing silence hummed between us until Tom said, "Vanessa wants you and Pax to have the baby."

I felt a hard tug in my stomach. "I'm sorry, what?"

"You know Vanessa has no inclination to become a mother. Her intention from the moment she found out about the pregnancy was to carry the baby to full term for you and Pax." Tom's words sucked the breath out of me. With the hairs on the back of my neck standing on end, our eyes held for a long moment. "She hasn't said anything to you because she wants to wait until she passes the critical period...and until she summoned the courage to talk to her parents."

Tom waited a beat for me to say something, and when I didn't he went on. "It was the reason we were out tonight. Vanessa had me put on a Christmas dinner for her parents at my place so she could talk to them about turning the baby over to you and Pax for adoption. She felt my place was neutral ground where she could talk to them openly. She also wanted me to be by her side for moral support, and as her legal counsel, when she divulged her plans to them.

She wanted me to assure them that I'd draft an agreement, which would ensure they would remain completely involved in the baby's life although she knew you and Pax would never deny them their grandparent's rights. That you'd both be more than willing to accept those terms since you'd understand that it would be difficult for her parents to surrender the baby to you. After all, it was going to be their first and, more than likely, only grandchild.

Her mother resisted the idea at first, offering to take responsibility for the baby, but her dad quickly got her to dismiss the notion by pointing out that in their mid-sixties they were too old to be caring for a baby. It took some doing, but eventually Vanessa and I got them to agree that having you adopt the baby was the best alternative." Tom looked from me to Pax as he spoke. "They and Vanessa signed the papers earlier this evening. So whether she comes out of this or…the baby is legally yours, Natalia."

My heart gave an involuntary leap and began pounding in my chest. I fell into a stunned silence, my emotions teetering on the edge of a tall mountain like a boulder waiting for that single push. I'd always been grateful to have a friend like Vanessa, but at that moment, my heart bloomed with love for her. Never in my wildest dreams did I imagine anyone doing what she was doing for me.

"Are you all right, sweets?" Pax asked, and that was when I covered my face with my hands and the tears came with guttural sobs.

"She can't leave me now. She just can't." I stared at Pax through the flood of tears, and he took me into a much-needed embrace.

"And she won't. No one is stronger than she is." Pax's reassuring eyes looked at me from beneath dark lashes.

For a long while, I cried tears of joy for the life Vanessa selflessly carried for me while consumed by an overwhelming sadness for the friend I stood to lose. I couldn't imagine having to come to terms with Vanessa not being in my life.

Suddenly, I felt completely drained. "I'm so tired."

Pulling me in closer, he kissed me on the forehead. As we shared in the tender moment, I watched Tom head for the door.

"Tom," I called out. When he turned to face me, I saw the depth of his pain in his eyes. The baby Vanessa carried wasn't his and now he stood to lose her. Walking over to him, I took him in a gentle embrace. "I'm so sorry, Tom. I wish it could all be different."

"Me too."

Thirty-One

DECEMBER CAME AND went, and, before I knew it, January was upon us and I was due back at work. I couldn't, however, in good conscience go back to the routine of a normal life. Nothing in my life then felt normal or routine. My sister's conversation about my father and Michael and their infidelity was still fresh on my mind as were the photographs she'd shown me. Pax fired Nora and replaced her with a male assistant immediately after I told him about her extracurricular activities. The shame of her betrayal to Pax and the affair, consumed her enough that she packed up and moved across country overnight. I knew that wouldn't stop Michael from taking on a new love interest, but it did improve my relationship with my sister.

We buried Vanessa's parents in what I hoped was a resting place they and Vanessa would approve of. Although there was so much going on then, my mind at times became curiously blank. It was during those moments when the feelings of complete helplessness washed over me and I felt as if my life was suspended in a nightmare with no end in sight.

I decided to take a leave of absence from work in order to care for Vanessa.

For the second time, I looked into my children's faces and announced that I would be taking an indefinite leave. Explaining as best I could to seven-year-olds that I was taking it in order to care for my sick friend was a task in itself.

A teary-eyed Maxine piped up. "How long will your friend be sick, Mrs. Reed?"

"I'm not sure, honey," I told the inquisitive doe-eyed girl staring up at me.

Tommy puffed his chest out like a peacock in an attempt to conceal the tears on the verge of flowing, but his unsteady tone said it all. "But...but Mrs. Reed, who's...who's going to help me with my reading?"

"Mrs. Stetson, the school librarian, will, sweetie. I've already spoken to her about it, and she's more than happy to spend one-on-one time with you." When Tommy began to pout, I said, "She loves cowboy stories as much as you and I do." His disappointed expression was quickly replaced with a wide grin.

After a thoughtful moment, Suzie spoke. "What's wrong with your friend, Mrs. Reed?"

In the simplest terms, I knew how, I explained. "Her brain is asleep right now and she needs someone to take care of her."

"Can we help you, Mrs. Reed? If we help you, then maybe you can stay with us." Suzie's offer got a nod of agreement from everyone.

"That's sweet of you, of all of you, and thank you for offering, but I need you to stay here and learn all you can so you can move on to grade three next year." When the room went silent, I added, "How about for art hour, we work on a giant get-well card for my friend Vanessa?" To my relief, my suggestion got approvals all around.

"Let's draw a giant yellow flower to cheer Mrs. Reed's friend up," Maxine suggested. "They always cheer me up."

Tommy soon after chimed in with, "We should draw a red car. Does your friend like red, Mrs. Reed?"

"I'll print my name on the card," Mindy volunteered, then added, "Like we do when we make the Mother's Day card."

Warmed by their enthusiasm, I flashed the children a smile. "Thank you. I think those are all wonderful ideas, and I know my friend will love it."

Thirty-Two

OVER THE NEXT few weeks, I was by Vanessa's side from dawn until dusk tending to her every need. The ongoing visits from Dr. Steward and the nurses, the cacophony of sounds from the machines, the interminable beeps of Vanessa's heart monitor, the only sign of life in her, was second nature to me now. With each passing week, through the miracle of science, there was a life growing in her listless body. I found myself mesmerized by the growth of her belly. There were days when I took pleasure at the thought of the baby inside her, and the promise of something new and exciting to come. Many were the days when I thought of the child inside her as the greatest blessing in my life and I already loved that baby more than life itself. But those blissful thoughts were often overshadowed by guilt and remorse, heartache and sadness. How could I justifiably be so happy when the woman who held that life, didn't have her own? Not really.

On her eighteenth week of pregnancy, Dr. Steward, asked me to rest my hand on Vanessa's belly. Initially, there was reluctance on my part. Partly out of fear for becoming too attached to the baby I wasn't entirely sure would be alive tomorrow, and partly because it felt as an intrusive act on my part. Once Dr. Steward took my hand and set it down on Vanessa's belly, I couldn't pull away. There was life there. Feeling the baby's movements was the most joyous sensation I'd experienced, and at that moment in time, I felt more closely connected with that baby than I ever had. I let my hand rest on Vanessa's belly for longer than I should have, but I couldn't seem to break the bond.

For as long as I lived, I knew I would forever remember and cherish that moment.

The weeks that followed were difficult on Vanessa. Her body was starting to show signs of medical complications. The most recent being a bladder infection, which I was told was due to the prolonged use of a catheter. I was assured that the antibiotics Dr. Steward prescribed to fight the infection would address the issue and not affect the baby.

On her bad days, I stayed with Vanessa overnight, sleeping on the cot the critical care staff set up in her room for me. And lately I was sleeping over a lot. I spent whatever time I could spare at the library, delving through medical books to educate myself on Vanessa's condition. On weekends, Pax came with me to the hospital and we both sat by Vanessa's bedside, reading to her, or simply talking about our week and including Vanessa in the conversation as if she was there with us. There were times when I believed she heard every word we said.

As word spread of Vanessa's condition, friends and co-workers—not surprisingly mainly of the male gender—began to trickle in and out of her room and not a day went by when the two of us were alone. It made me happy to see how much Vanessa was loved, and how many lives she touched.

Tom came by to see Vanessa often, and we'd pass the time sharing our memories of her. In time, I came to understand how deeply in love he was with her. When I found out Tom never told Vanessa how he truly felt, I encouraged him to do so.

"Even in her comatose state, they say she hears us and I know she would love to hear how you feel for her, Tom." I told him often enough that in time, he opened up to Vanessa, and soon after I sensed the debilitating grief that was consuming him tapered off to a dull pain.

Through our love for Vanessa, Tom and I eventually became good friends, relying on each other for comfort and support. And we both knew it was as Vanessa would have wanted it.

Thirty-Three

MARCH BREEZED IN with the newness of life, the greenness of the new season, and the scent of flowers in bloom. Streams of gold from a morning sun seeped through the windows of Vanessa's hospital room, hitting the white-tiled floor and dispersing into a prism of light and hope.

Combing Vanessa's hair, I clamped it back with a hair clip. "Dr. Steward says you're doing well and so is the baby. It's a little girl. I know I've told you all this before, and knowing you as well as I do, I know you're chastising me for sounding like a broken record. Well, get used to it, because I'm never going to stop talking about her. And I'm never going to stop thanking you either, because I want you to know how grateful Pax and I are for what you're doing for us. Having this baby is the greatest act of love for Pax and me. I never in a million years imagined anyone would do anything so selfless for us. I like to think I would have done the exact thing for you if the roles were reversed. I know I've said all this to you many times before, but get used to me telling you again and again how complete you've made my life by giving me such a precious gift.

We've decided we're going to name her Vanessa Marigold Roberts-Reed. I know it's a mouthful, but I wanted Marigold in her name in memory of your mother, and she of course must carry your last name. We'll be calling the baby Nessi, so no one gets confused between you and her. I can already picture her having your exotic looks, and I pray that she'll have your firecracker personality and be as compassionate and kind as you are." As I spoke, I sensed Pax and Tom listening from the doorway.

"Hi." Pax joined me bedside, while Tom replaced the week-old roses in the vase with a bouquet of spring flowers.

"How's she doing today?" Tom asked, setting the flowers on her bedside table.

"Wonderfully. I think she really likes it when I talk to her. Sometimes, in the middle of a story I can feel her squeezing my hand." I watched him curl his hand around Vanessa's.

"I'm sure she does, and I bet you she does it more so when you're gossiping with her." Tom playfully winked at me.

"Why Mr. Webster, are you insinuating we gossip?" I caught Tom's raised brow, but it was Pax who braved to answer the question.

"Gossip and shoe shopping. Isn't that why women have been put on this earth?" Pax looked to Tom for confirmation.

"It's a brave man who says that out loud, and I'm not that man so I'm going to plead the fifth on this one." Tom rushed to say, and as Pax and I burst into laughter I was certain Vanessa squeezed my hand then. "Do we know why Dr. Steward called us in today?"

I shook my head. "I guess it's because Vanessa's nearing the twenty-week pregnancy mark," I said picking up the vase of flowers to refresh the water under the tap in the bathroom. "They're beautiful, Tom. Vanessa loves spring flowers."

Tom nodded knowingly. "Daisies are her favorite."

I should have known better than to assume he didn't. The man knew Vanessa inside and out and I thought she was so lucky to have him in her life. He had been there by her side day and night, racked with worry.

"Twenty-weeks is a milestone," Tom said.

"I'd say so, and Natalia is probably right about Dr. Steward wanting to update us on her status. She's been really good all these months about keeping us in the loop." Pax took my hand, curled his fingers tightly around it.

"She mentioned something about legalities. She was vague, but I think she wants to discuss that with you and Tom."

At the sound of Dr. Steward's voice approaching Vanessa's room, we turned toward the door.

"Thank you for coming, and it's nice to see all of you again, although you and I are now on a first-name basis." She flashed me the familiar smile. "I wanted to have a discussion with you about baby Nessi. I understand that's what you've named her." Dr. Steward turned to Pax and me, and we both nodded. "As of today, Vanessa is entering her twentieth week of pregnancy, which as you know, means that in four weeks baby Nessi will have a good chance of survival outside of the womb. Having passed the critical mark, I think we need to carefully consider our next step."

"How's that, doctor?" I asked.

Dr. Steward turned to me. "I'd like you to give some serious thought as to whether we should deliver baby Nessi at the twenty-fourth week."

"What are you saying, Dr. Steward?" I asked.

"I'm sorry, but I need to be blunt right now. Vanessa is in a prolonged state of unconsciousness, unresponsive to her environment, and kept alive by a series of machines. All indication is that Vanessa will not wake from her comatose state. Worse than that, the baby is demanding too much from her. I want you to consider delivering Nessi in four weeks."

The shock hit me like a swift punch to the stomach. "Are you saying we need to choose between Vanessa and the baby?"

Dr. Steward nodded. "Unfortunately, I am. Vanessa has endured significant neurological injury and deregulation of major body systems. Although she's stable now, we can't predict how her brain and body will react at any given moment. And as the baby continues to grow, she will demand more of Vanessa. We're not sure how those additional stresses will affect Vanessa or Nessi."

We lapsed into a lifeless silence, as we considered the magnitude of her statement. She was asking us to choose between Vanessa and the baby. We were being asked to choose a life for a death. How did you choose between your best friend's life and that of your baby's?

I fell into a silent, vacant world of darkness.

"What's your professional opinion, Dr. Steward?" Pax asked.

"No one at this hospital, including myself, has ever faced a case like Vanessa's, but after consulting with my colleagues here and at hospitals around the country, the general consensus is that since we're nearing the safe point in the pregnancy where we should deliver baby Nessi sooner than later."

Dr. Steward's voice calm and soothing didn't prevent the Anxiety from stabbing at the center of my chest. "Isn't there a chance Vanessa can come out of this?"

Dr. Steward rested a hand on mine. "I'm afraid not, Natalia."

I felt the tears burning in the back of my eyes. "What are Nessi's chances of survival if you deliver her in four weeks?" I asked and immediately felt the pang of guilt at the question.

Cautiously, Dr. Steward proceeded. "The baby is strong and she appears to be healthy. She's still small, probably under three pounds, but if she's as resilient as her mother, she'll require neonatal care for only a short period of time and be home sooner than you think."

"I've heard of comatose patients waking up after years of being on life support." Tom's voice broke.

"We will do everything possible to ensure her well-being. As I said, she's resilient and definitely a fighter, I'll give her that. But with so many unknowns, I couldn't give you any assurances that there won't be complications during the delivery. There is a high probability that Vanessa may not make it," Dr. Steward said point blank.

The words came out so fast, I wasn't sure I'd heard them right. The room suddenly felt suffocating as the implications of her words became clear. This nightmare seemed to have no ending. I felt as if I was on a rollercoaster of despair that didn't seem to want to come to a stop. Paralyzed with fear, I thought of Nessi, and of Vanessa, who had been a part of my life since I could remember. I flashed back to the memories of our long talks and our visits together. I thought back to that first day we'd met, and every important event we'd shared since then flashed in my mind.

We'd made plans, so many plans, and I couldn't bear the thought of Vanessa not being in my life to fulfill them with me. Particularly now that she had given us the most wonderful gift—Nessi, the child I could never have.

Suddenly I felt anxious. I tried to tell myself that this was all a mistake, that Dr. Steward didn't know what she was talking about. But as hard as I tried to ignore the reality of the situation, the sinking feeling in my stomach wouldn't allow it. This whole conversation was as real as the incessant beeps from the machines in the room keeping Vanesa alive. Although I knew she was trapped in a body that gave her no choice but to be in the distressed state she was in, I wanted her to will it better, for her, for me, for Tom. For the baby to come.

"There's one additional cog to this complicated wheel that I must burden you with," Dr. Steward set apologetic eyes on us. "Nessi is yours, Natalia, there's no disputing that. But until she's delivered she's Vanessa's child, which means you have no legal standing to make medical decisions on her behalf. And since Vanessa has no family left, we will need to request the courts to appoint someone as a guardian ad litem to make medical decisions for her." Her Goddamn beeper went off. This time Dr. Steward ignored it.

"Jesus! So everything we've discussed, everything you've told us is moot. What we want has no bearing on anything. This...this guardian ad litem will be making all decisions. This conversation has been completely useless," I lashed out in frustration.

If Dr. Steward was offended by the remark, she didn't show it. "Don't look at it that way, Natalia. Nessi is your baby, and I wanted your input, which I plan to pass on to her guardian. I've found them amenable in the past." Dr. Steward rose to her five-nine height. "I know it's a lot of information to digest, and I'm aware that this is difficult for you, but I'd rather you were kept informed." She turned to Pax and Tom. "With both of you being lawyers, I was hoping you could assist in expediting this through the courts."

Pax who had been silent said now, "One question, Dr. Steward. If a blood relative, let's say the baby's father, was to come forward, he would have the right to make all the medical decisions?"

"Yes, that's my understanding. But I thought you didn't know who the father was."

"You know who the father is?" I kept my eyes direct on Pax. "You've known all along?"

Pax glanced sideways at me, then away. His face contorted in angst, his blue eyes blinked erratically, and thrusting his hands deep into his jeans pocket, he flickered apologetic eyes at me then, to Tom. For a long silent moment, our eyes held as he considered his response. My mind clouded, it took me some time before I focused and was able to read his face. When I followed the thread to its logical conclusion and saw with perfect clarity, the air clogged my lungs.

"Oh, my God. It's yours. You're Nessi's father."

Thirty-Four

PAX DIDN'T SEE Tom's fist coming. When it connected with Pax's jaw, the crunch of bone on bone was nauseating. Pax's eyes widened in shock, his head tilted back, and he stumbled for a brief second before he managed to right himself. When he did you could hear him wheezing, struggling to get the air knocked out of back him into his lungs.

"You son of a bitch." Tom's eyes filled with fury and determination, he lunged a second tight fisted punch, but he managed to evade that one.

Pax wiped his hand across the corner of his mouth where he'd tasted blood. "Let me explain, Tom,"

The anger laced string of oaths that followed from Tom drew a group of curious onlookers outside Vanessa's room.

"There's nothing you could say that I'd want to hear from you, you fucking asshole. I thought you were my friend. You knew how I felt about her. You knew I loved her." Tom launched another punch. This time with more anger, and what seemed a gleam of madness in his eyes. Pax was quick enough to dodge that one too.

"It's not what you think." A fine spray of blood from Pax's mouth came when he spoke.

"Take your punches like a man, you fucking bastard." The muscles on Tom's jaw quivered.

"I would if I thought I deserved them," Pax said darting right and left to avoid Tom's relentless punches.

I couldn't understand his rationalisation. He'd slept with Vanessa, my best friend and the woman Tom loved. How did he think he could justify betraying both of us? I watched Tom throw another tight-fisted punch and decided this wasn't the time to think things through. "That's enough," I cried out stepping between them.

"Fine." Fists clenched at Tom's side.

"You step back." I motioned Pax to one corner of the room to put distance between them.

When she determined it was safe, Dr. Steward walked over to Pax.

"It's a minor cut," Dr. Steward said after examining the blood pooling at Pax's puffy lip. "One of my nurses will take care of it."

Pax clasped his jaw between his thumb and forefinger, and shifted it back and forth. "I'm fine, thank you."

"All right, but if you need that looked after, you know where to find Mary. In the meantime, she'll get you an ice pack." Dr. Steward told Tom. "Are you all right?"

"I'm fine," Tom said flexing his hand and appearing seemingly satisfied by the sting on his knuckles.

"You should put some ice on that too. Now, no more fighting on my ward. You want to act like children you take it elsewhere." With unwavering eyes, Dr. Steward waited for Tom and Pax's nod before walking out of the room and dispersing the gawking group.

Treachery and betrayal slapping me in the face I said, "How could you do this to me, to Tom?"

"It's not what you think," Pax said wiping blood from his lips with the tissue Mary handed him.

I put the much-needed distance between us. "Stupid me. I thought all the interest you were expressing for Vanessa was because you were starting to warm to her. I never in a million years imagined it was because.... How long have you been warming her bed? Days, weeks, months, years? How long have you, and her, been making a fool of me? Do you know how much you've hurt me?" I felt the tears forming in my eyes, but I fought against them. I'd cry buckets on my own. I wouldn't cry them in front of Pax. I couldn't give him the satisfaction.

"It's not like that, Natalia. You need to let me explain. Please, Natalia. Please, Tom, you need to hear me out." He reached for my hand, but I jolted back.

Feeling the need to put miles of distance between myself and Pax, I turned to Tom and said, "Will you take me home?"

Tom raked mussed hair back from his eyes. "Of course, Natalia. You can stay at my place if you like. For as long as you want." His tone was ripe with macho intimation.

I dismissed the insolent comment as projected anger toward Pax. "Thank you, but I'll be fine at my place. I need to get out of here now."

"Let's go," Tom said resting a hand on my back more out of spite than chivalry.

"Wait, you have to let me explain," Pax called after us.

At the door, Tom stopped and held up a hand. "You have nothing to say that I'm interested in hearing, and I'm certain Natalia feels the same."

Words I never thought I'd say to Pax tumbled out with an anger I didn't think I had in me. "I not only not want to listen to anything you have to say, but I can't even stand to be in the same room as you. I can't stand to look at you. And don't think of coming home tonight," or ever I wanted to add, but I couldn't bring myself to say it.

Every man in my family seemed to want to find comfort in the arms of another woman. I never imagined it would touch my marriage. I'd told myself that often enough after the unpleasant conversation with Caterina that I'd come to believe it. Yet here I was hit by the ultimate betrayal. The two people I loved most, I trusted with my life, my husband and my best friend, had found comfort in one another's arms.

THERE WAS A RELENTLESS DEBILITATING ACHE that went bone deep and kept me away from Pax and the hospital for days. Every waking day I thought of Nessi. I ached to rest my hand on Vanessa's swelling belly and feel the life in her, but I couldn't bring myself to be in the same room as Vanessa. There were also days when my hatred— although I suspected it was more pain and the feeling of betrayal—for Pax and Vanessa ran so deep that I wanted nothing to do with Nessi.

Nessi was their child, not mine.

The wrenching sense of loss of Nessi, and Pax, and my best friend was overwhelming, but I didn't cry. I refused to.

I slept in the guest room to avoid Pax's scent, which was everywhere and was a constant reminder of the man I loved and his infidelity. I didn't dare get into the bed we'd shared, where he'd made me believe in love, and told me I was the only woman he would ever love. Where he'd whispered secrets in my ears, which now meant nothing. The pain that lanced me was like no pain I'd ever known. It clawed at me like an animal at its dead prey.

On my secluded back deck hemmed by the forest of majestic trees rising tall, I spent most of my days sheltered from the world. Today the sun was high in a fierce blue sky, and the spring twitter of birds sounded from trees crowned in a canopy of splendid green. The air, infused with the scents of earth and pine, smelled fresh. I thought of how many weekends Pax and I had spent out here in conversation with a nice glass of wine. A cold chill tripped down my spine at the notion that there would be no such shared moments—ever again.

How could I ever trust Pax again? I'd never believe anything he said again, and doubted everything he had. Anger and disappointment, hurt and despair, all seemed to wash over me at once.

I whipped my head up when the familiar scent flowed into me. My heart sprang to my throat when I saw him standing at the French doors. His eyes shadowed with dark circles were hard to miss. His jaw hadn't seen a razor for days. Today being Saturday Pax was dressed casual: running shoes, a Black Sabbath T-shirt, and jeans. The latter two could have used a hot iron, and yet he still had that fierce handsome look that had drawn me to him.

There was love for him still in me. I felt it strong in me. It was more than I anticipated. For a fleeting moment I wanted to smile, to fall into his arms and let him hold me, but I fought the urge.

"I should have changed the lock like Tom told me to," I said.

Pax's shoulders tensed. "Tom's staying here with you?"

I didn't dignify the question with a response. "What are you doing here, Pax?"

He jammed his hands deep into his jeans pockets, and stared down at his feet. "I hoped we could talk."

"We have nothing to talk about." I turned my back to him.

"We do, Natalia. You have to let me explain."

I turned to face him. "What's there to explain? What could you possibly say that could fix this, fix us? You slept with my best friend. Do you know how humiliated and betrayed I feel? Do you know how much you've hurt me? No, you couldn't possibly because I would never betray you. I would never give you cause to feel as you've made me feel." There was enough bite in my words to show my anger, and let him recognize how much I did hurt.

He stepped closer. When I held my hand up he stopped. "I would never betray you, Natalia. I love you."

I wanted to cry, but my anger took over. "You have a warped sense of the meaning of love." I found myself reaching for the non-existent glass of brandy. Jesus, I needed a drink.

"Hear me out, Natalia." He moved over to one of the apple-red Muskoka chairs and when I said nothing he sat down.

"I don't totally blame you for what you did. I know I wasn't woman enough for you."

"Don't say that. I never once thought of you in that way."

I raised my face against the strength of the sun. "I can't give you the family you want, and deep down I imagined you'd eventually turn to someone who could. But I never imagined you'd turn to Vanessa. My best friend, Pax. It would have been less painful if you'd taken up with a stranger, or better yet, if you'd taken me up on my offer to opt out of this marriage when I offered you the opportunity to do so, so you could find yourself a…complete woman. At least it would have been on my terms. I trusted you and Vanessa as I've never trusted before. I shared my pain and my tears, my love with both of you." The tears I'd been holding off for days flowed, buckets of them.

"Please, don't…don't cry, Natalia," he said, his voice panicked.

Fighting to keep the tears from blurring my vision, I looked up at him. "Did you point a finger at Michael to distract me from what you and Vanessa were doing? How long was it going on? No, don't answer that. I don't want to know."

"We did what we did for you, Natalia."

I let out a derisive laugh. "That's rich. 'Oh, by the way I rolled in the sheets with your best friend for your benefit.' Really, Pax." Wiping my eyes dry, I got to my feet. "I'm here to pick up the last of my things. I'm moving back in with my parents. This is your home, not mine. I want no connection to it, to you, or anything that relates to you." I didn't imagine it would be so difficult to say those words.

Pax wasn't expecting that, and he sank to his knees beside me, the tears pouring from his eyes. "No, don't say that, Natalia. You can't leave me."

I set my house key on the rail, and started to walk away.

"Vanessa wanted to have a baby for you, Natalia." He blurted out quick and swift like pulling off a Band-Aid.

"You were hurting so much, Natalia, shutting yourself away, without realizing it. You were so…so very sad. I'd hear you crying in the shower. I'd hear you whimpering next to me in bed late at night. I'd see your eyes puffed and red when I came home from work." The sun streaming over his tilted face made his teary eyes glint.

I opened my mouth to stop him talking, but he plowed on.

"Then anger began to consume you. You became bitter, resentful and cynical of everyone and everything. You dismissed my suggestion for adoption saying that you wanted nothing to do with a child that wasn't ours. That you could never have feelings for a child that wasn't of our blood or that had no relationship to us. You looked so broken and unhappy, Natalia, and I couldn't stand to see you like that. I know that your recovery from the…experience would be a lifelong process, but you were hurting so much I couldn't simply stand by feeling helpless.

So, when Vanessa came to me with the crazy scheme it wasn't that difficult for her to talk me into it. I wouldn't normally have, but you were in so much pain, depressed for months after the doctor told you you'd never be able to have a baby that I let her. For you. You're the most important person in the world to me, and it killed me to see you so unhappy. I know what we did was wrong, and we should have told you. We should have told you. I wanted to tell you," he repeated, raking fingers through his hair. "But she told me you'd never agree to it. And again I allowed her to lead the way. I know this all sounds crazy, but it's the truth, Natalia."

"Let me see. You're excuse for sleeping with my best friend was to conceive a child for me? How very noble of you and her."

"It's God's truth, Natalia. I was very much against it at first, I tried to steer her to Tom or even Michael to…you know. Only because I'd seen Michael pursuing her for some time," he said when my eyes widened. "I vowed to her I'd never divulge the identity of the baby's father once she turned her over to us. But when she told me how much Tom wanted children, I couldn't do that to him. And as for Michael, well, I retracted the suggestion the moment I spit it out. Everything I'm telling you is God's honest truth." The sincerity in his eyes jangled at my female sensibilities, and something squeezed inside me and began to cloud my judgement.

"Jesus! This all sounds…" I started to speak, but Pax quickly cut me off.

"Like a fantastic tale. I know, but it's not. It's the honest truth. There was no emotion involved. It was all clinical. Natalia, she risked her relationship with Tom for this. She told me she loved him, and she hoped this wouldn't change things between them. She prayed he'd understand when she told him it was something she needed to do for you. I too prayed that you'd understand it was something I did for you."

All I could think to say was, "I need a drink."

"I'll get it for you," he said and headed into the kitchen. A few minutes later he came back with two glasses of scotch. "I thought you'd need something stronger than wine."

"I don't know how to process all this. I don't even know where to begin." I took the offered glass and drank deep.

Pax drank with me. "I know."

"I need time."

"Understood." He drank more scotch and I did too. "I wanted…needed you to know the truth. You believe me?"

I fell into a long silence as I considered, and he waited it out. "I do."

He stared at me. "Are you okay?"

"No, I'm not. Maybe in time I will be."

"Are we okay?"

I tilted my face up to his. "I don't know."

Thirty-Five

AFTER MY CONVERSATION with Pax I moved into my parent's. Although I believed every word of his fantastic story, I couldn't come to terms with him and Vanessa sleeping together. I needed to put distance between Pax and me. I needed time to think, and sort the tangled thoughts in my head.

Did he love her?

How many times had they come together?

Where had they…?

When had they come together? Was I at work, was it on the weekends Pax told me he was at work?

Had he kissed her the way he did me?

Pax telephoned every day, but I refused to take his calls. Then, the letters started coming sometimes twice daily. When I returned them, he began to show up at my parent's door to be turned away. Each time, from behind the white lace curtains at my bedroom window I watched him, as shoulders slumped and head bowed, he made his way back to his car. And each time I wished I could dart out and chain my arms around him and tell him that I forgave him that everything would be fine. But the bitter taste of his betrayal still strong on my tongue, I did nothing but watch him drive away until the car faded in the distance.

I couldn't sleep most nights, going over Pax's story in my head. Would the pain and the heartache stabbing at me ever fade? Would I forgive Pax? Should I forgive Pax? Was this going to lead to the end of my marriage? Would I never feel his arms around me? Would I forget the taste of his love? And what was to become of Nessi? I loved her, and felt a terrible ache every day I wasn't by her side. But she wasn't my child. She was theirs.

My once perfect life had spiraled out of control in a matter of days. I didn't know what to make of everything I felt. Many days I felt as if I was standing at the center of a maze that spiraled into itself.

I was at an impasse.

The days passed in a blur, turning into weeks. It would be four of them from the time of our conversation before I'd come face to face with Pax, and only because of the unexpected call from Dr. Steward summoning us to the hospital.

I hadn't seen Vanessa in as long, and I wasn't sure what to expect. When I walked into her room, it was eerily silent. There was no audible puff of air from the ventilator. There were no beeps from her heart monitor. The machines flashing her heart rate and blood pressure were turned off. The silence sent a chill through me.

"Where is she?" I asked Tom.

Standing at the window, Tom lifted his head to the sky as lightning slashed and flashed. Through the rumble of thunder, the rain lashed, torrential, and unforgiving, slamming against the windowpane. The patter of rain striking the window filled the silence in the room.

"She's suffered a cerebral aneurysm and was rushed into surgery." His voice was soft.

"When?"

Streaks of lightning flashed across the sky, thunder followed and more rain, wild and furious, poured.

Tom turned. I could tell he'd been crying. "She's been doing really well. She'd even gone beyond the twenty-four-week mark. They thought she would go well beyond that. I thought she would. I thought she may even come out of her coma. I know it was a stretch, but she's a fighter, you know." His eyes were focused out the window.

"When did they take her down, Tom?"

"A couple of hours ago. I was reading to her, and…"

"Is she going to be okay?"

"I don't know. They don't know."

"And Nessi?" I had to ask.

Tom fell back onto the window ledge. "She and Nessi's life are both at risk. They may not…"

"Oh, God!" The room began to spin, and my legs gave up on me. Tom rushed to catch me before I hit tiled floor. As Tom scooped me in his arms, from the corner of my eyes I saw Pax. He stood framed in the doorway. He said nothing. His eyes on Tom were unwavering and dark.

"Don't just stand there. Get her some water," Tom called out to Pax.

In seconds, Pax was by my side holding a small Dixie cup to my lips. "Drink some water, Natalia."

Looking up at Pax I did. There was so much emotion stirring in his eyes. I could see the same pain and despair that had ripped at my heart in them. There was hurt, and sadness, and regret. And there was love. The true, all-encompassing love he'd promised to share with me all of his life. I was drowning in it.

"If you're okay, Natalia, I'll be down the hall, in the waiting room," Tom said eyeing Pax with disdain.

Pulling away from his arms, I called out to Tom. "Please, Tom, stay."

Tom's mouth tightened briefly. "I'm sorry, Natalia, but I can't stand to be in the same room with him."

"That's okay I'll leave." Pax headed toward the door. "You can stay here with Natalia."

"Get out of my way, Reed. I'm leaving," Tom said bulldozing his way past Pax.

I felt the muscles in my stomach tighten. My world was falling apart. Pax and Tom were at each other's throats. I wanted to put distance between the man I still loved more than life itself and me. Vanessa and Nessi were on an operating table fighting for their lives.

"No. No one is leaving."

The anger in my tone made both of them stop in their tracks. "This isn't the time for ill will or hatred. Today is not about you or you or me. It's about Vanessa and Nessi who may not come out of this operation alive. "Both of you plant your asses down. We're waiting here together. I mean it. Now, sit your asses down."

Without argument Pax and Tom did as told although they remained as far apart from one another as possible. No one said anything, and in silence we waited together for news on Vanessa and Nessi.

WITH HER TEAM BY HER SIDE, Dr. Steward spent hours in surgery, and whether through the virtues of modern medicine or divine intervention, Vanessa survived the operation, and the life inside her came through unscathed.

Vanessa's window of survival, however, quickly closed in on her again, and before the surgical gloves were off, she was rushed back to the operating theater. This time however, Dr. Steward was compelled to make the daunting decision of whether to save Vanessa's or Nessi's life.

Pax, as Nessi's father, was consulted, or more directly to the point, told what was about to take place because in the end there was but one option available.

One hour later, Vanessa Marigold Roberts-Reed was born via caesarean section at a meagre three pounds, two ounces, but healthy otherwise. Vanessa, who had surrendered her life for her baby's well-being, lay lifeless on the operating table.

THE MOMENT THE NURSE SET NESSI down in my arms, the room filled with oxygen. I fell under her spell. Holding that wiggling bundle of joy as those dark eyes looked up at me made my heart swell with pure love, and in my eyes, there was nothing more special and beautiful than her. She righted a world, which in the past few months had tilted on its axis. The world suddenly narrowed down to this beautiful three-pound bundle in my arms. She erased the heartache, the pain, the misery. She filled me with pure joy, and she was all that mattered, and I knew I would go to the ends of the earth to ensure that little girl's safety and happiness.

She had Pax's eyes, and mouth. The mass of dark hair was Vanessa's as were the long, graceful fingers. And I had to attribute the piercing wail to Vanessa. She was beautiful, and I didn't doubt she would go on to break many hearts.

When her tiny fingers curled around my pinky as if latching onto me, I felt a symbiotic connection. She was mine and I was hers.

TOGETHER TOM, PAX AND I WAITED outside Vanessa's room to see her for one last time and say our goodbyes. At that moment, there was no anger, no animosity, no bitterness toward one another. There was only love flowing through us for Vanessa.

The wait to see Vanessa felt like an eternity.

It was some time before Mary led us in. A still, chilling silence hung in the room and my eyes were immediately drawn to the still body. A white bed sheet matching her sallow complexion was pulled up to her shoulders. I reached to touch her, hoping to wake her, hoping to infuse her with life, but she was cold. So cold. A helpless grief welled up in my heart at seeing the luster in her eyes gone for good, the life in her faded. I fell into Pax and he held me, and tried to comfort me as I cried for the friend I loved and lost.

Lightning slashed and flashed outside painting the sky with short flickers of light and I wondered if it was her making her grand entry into heaven.

"I'm so sorry for not being here with you on your last days. Thank you for being my friend and touching my life as you did. And most of all thank you for the beautiful gift you leave behind. I love you, Vanessa, and I'll never forget you. And I promise you that Nessi will know you and I'll make sure she carries the memory of you with her all of her life." Across from me, Tom's tears slid through closed lashes in silence as he tenderly kissed Vanessa on the lips and whispered, "Until we meet again my love."

Pax kissed Vanessa on the forehead and told her that she would always live in our memory, and in Nessi.

It was hard to imagine I'd never see or talk to her again. Visions of Vanessa throughout the life we'd shared began to swim in my head with a clarity that surprised me. I saw us in my bedroom, in our purple girl-power nightgowns at our first sleepover, making plans. So many plans. I visualized us on graduation day, walking on stage to accept our diplomas. I vividly pictured us walking down the boardwalk in the Beaches and having dinner at The Bistro. The vision of her beautiful smile came to me as she sashayed down the aisle and stood next to me when Pax and I exchanged wedding vows. I remembered the many times she'd stood on the other side of my front door, hot and sweaty after her runs. But most of all, I remembered how she'd always been there for me when I needed a friend, and I was so grateful that she had been a part of my life.

I prayed then, that the memories and her image would never fade from my mind.

I kissed Vanessa on the cheek, before I squeezed my eyes shut and said a silent goodbye to the friend I deeply love and would desperately miss.

IT WAS LATE EVENING WHEN WE left the hospital. The rain had stopped, and although it was mid-May, there was now a chill in the night air. Standing between Pax and Tom, I held their hands as we silently walked back to our cars.

When Tom started toward his car, I pulled him in. "You shouldn't be alone right now."

"I'm fine, Natalia." Tom turned misted eyes to me.

"You're not. None of us are. You're coming home with me and Pax, and you're staying with us for as long as you want," I said giving Tom's hand a squeeze.

Pax's eyebrows winged up. "You're coming home?"

I met his gaze and nodded. "All three of us need to be together now and we need to talk things out. You both need to talk things out." When I sensed Tom was about to voice a refusal, I quickly cut him off. "I know Vanessa would want us to be there for one another."

"She would," Tom said softly.

Thirty-Six

WHEN SOMEONE YOU love has died, everything changes. You see life through different eyes. Some view life in a more optimistic light, others, in a pessimistic way. Whatever your viewpoint, there's now a void in your life that will only be filled through memories, because death is the final exit.

Tom, Pax, and I decided to view Vanessa's death as we believed she would have wanted us to—optimistically. It was why we spent days talking things out, and, in the end, we resolved to work things out. Pax told Tom how Vanessa felt about him, and although it took some convincing, Tom eventually came to accept that Vanessa, not Pax, was instrumental in bringing them together, and only to conceive Nessi for me. I also accepted that as fact, not only because I came to believe it, but because Vanessa poured bright light into my sad existence and made me feel like the complete woman I thought I'd never be.

It would take some time for Tom's and my wounds to completely heal, but like it or not, the three of us were inextricably linked to Vanessa, and although she was the source of our pain, we loved her. Love always trumped anger.

Together, Tom, Pax and I made the funeral arrangements for Vanessa. It was our last gesture of love for her. It was when we'd bring all her friends together to celebrate her life, and it was what gave us real solace.

One week after Vanessa lost her long-fought battle, on a warm May day, under the sprinkle of a bright light from a glowing sun, she was buried at the Holy Trinity Cemetery alongside her parents.

With birds fluttering in the skies above us, chirping in symphony, Tom, Pax, and I, and hundreds of her friends, listened to the priest's last words. Everyone nodded in agreement when he said that Vanessa would live not only in her daughter Nessi, but also in our hearts. Mourners beamed with admiration when Father O'Malley pointed out the people whose lives Vanessa had enriched with the gift of sight, a healthy liver and her loving heart.

Shadowed-eyes, holding Pax and Tom's hand, I watched Vanessa's casket lowered into a darkness she would never come back from.

Friends and colleagues filed single line to offer us their condolences. Dr. Steward and many members of her critical care team came to say their goodbyes to the selfless woman who had only been a part of their lives for a short few months, but who they would not soon forget. Vanessa, to everyone who knew her, would forever be known as the woman who had given her life to give her friend the baby she couldn't have.

Thirty-Seven

I HAVE KNOWN love. The love of my parents, the love of a sibling, the love of a best friends, and the love of a man. Nothing however could ever compare to the love I felt for Nessi. It transcended every emotion I'd ever felt. It filled me with joy through the worst and the best of times. It gave my life meaning. It made my life worth living. I'd give my life for Nessi. She made me understand that she didn't have to come from me or that I should care how she came to be in this world, but that I should be grateful that she was a part of my life.

I watched Nessi run ahead of Pax and me with Doodle, the Yorkshire terrier Uncle Tom had given her last year for her eighth birthday, along with the pug she'd named Noodle that Pax showed up with last night and she fills me with an overwhelming joy. I wondered how I could have ever imagined rejecting her. Anger, I supposed, clouds your judgement and clinging to it was far simpler than dealing with the grief that was consuming me.

The grounds today are a luscious green. The smell of freshly cut grass along with the scent of flowers painted the air. Waves of color from the tulips, crocuses, asters and dahlias speared from the gardens throughout the property. Bees hummed around the wine-red rhododendrons, and the cheery tweeting sound of birds flowed from tree tops. It almost felt like a Disney production.

I waved to Mr. and Mrs. Gentry who visit their only son often, and to Mrs. Love and her son Gerald who is pushing her wheelchair along the pathway that winds throughout the property. Mr. O'Malley tips his checkered cap off before he went back to animatedly share his weekly going-ons with his wife. I smiled when I recalled him jokingly tell me, "It's the first time I'm able to get a word in edgewise."

"Really, Pax, a second dog. Isn't Goldy the gold fish, Nibbler the hamster and Meowsy the cat enough animals already?"

"It's what she wanted for her birthday," Pax countered, locking the car door.

"A seven-year-old has you wrapped around her little finger. So, if she asks for a Ferrari for her sixteenth birthday, I should anticipate one showing up on our driveway?"

"I wouldn't put it past me," he said and when I arched a brow, he proceeded to correct himself. "Okay, maybe a used Ford."

"Baby, keep close to Daddy and me. I'm going to have to keep a closer eye on you, Mr. Reed, because you are spoiling that little girl, and you will stop at nothing to give her everything she wants."

He turned to me with a wickedly smug smile. "Guilty as charged, but I enjoy spoiling her so. You're not going to deny me that, are you? I don't see her mother denying me the opportunity to spoil her when I do so." Pax pulled me in, and the tender brush of his lips against mine shot a flood of liquid heat through me. I loved the fact he could still make me feel that way.

Reveling in the sensation, it took a moment to answer him. "Don't try to sweet talk your way out of this."

With a tender touch, he brushed a strand of hair from my face. "Can't I kiss my beautiful wife?"

Suspicious, I looked him in the eyes. "You're up to something, aren't you?"

He pulled back from me. "I don't know what you're talking about."

"Sooner or later I'm going to find out, so you may as well come clean now."

Impish eyes drifted over to Nessi, who was attempting to put her sun hat on Doodle, and the dog obediently sat there letting her with Noodle watching on. "I don't know what you're talking about."

"Mmm-hmm. Are you going into work later today?"

"You know I wouldn't dare miss our daughter's birthday party. Besides, we still have a lot to do to get ready for the party. And I need to be at home when..." He shifted guilt-laden eyes away from me.

"When what, Pax? What did you promise Nessi now?"

"Nothing." He vehemently shook his head, which told me I should expect to be shocked.

"Pax?" I took note of the eyes that absently rolled. "What did you promise Nessi?"

"A pony," he finally fessed up, and proceeded to plead his case. "Bessie and Bob will be here at four. They're miniature ponies and will only be here for the duration of the birthday party." The words tumbled out faster than I could keep up.

"Ponies? Two of them?" I cried out, although nothing he did for Nessi at this point should have surprised me anymore. She was Daddy's little girl, had been since the moment he'd laid eyes on her, and although I wouldn't have wanted it any other way, we were now crossing the point of no return. Ponies, plural.

"We're not keeping them. I promise."

"I should hope not."

"So, you're okay with it? With Bessie and Bob...visiting."

I erupted into laughter. When I stopped I said, "Bessie and Bob can visit. This daughter of ours is going to become one out-of-control diva." Just then, the wind blew thick, dark curls over Nessi's eyes, and she brushed it back with a gesture that was so much like Vanessa's.

"I know, but it's so hard to say no to her." Pax broke into a smile of guiltless pleasure.

Nessi looked up at us with the smile that always clenched my heart. Like her mother, she had grown into an exquisite beauty. Large lake-blue eyes were set in an oval face the color of caramel. Her lips were a soft pink and her sculpted cheekbones were a ruddy red. Looking at Nessi always brought back memories of Vanessa.

Nessi waved her hands in the air for our attention. "Look, Mommy. Look, Daddy. See what I teached Noodle to do." When we turned to face her, she held out her hand, and the dog set his paw on it. When Noodles' tail animatedly swished in response to our praise, she giggled a beautiful girlish laugh.

"Very good, Baby, but it's what you taught Noodle to do." The teacher in me corrected her.

Nessi's nose wrinkled up the same way Vanessa used to when challenged, and just as Vanessa used to, considered before correcting herself. "Taught Noodle to do," she said, her eyes on me before they turned to Pax. "Daddy, will you help me find a stick for Doodle and Noodle to fetch?" She flashed the smile she knew could get Pax to do anything for her. She was her mother's daughter.

"Of course I will, Baby, but we can only play fetch after we finish visiting." Pax dashed ahead of me on command, and I couldn't help but laugh. She had him trained better than Noodle and Doodle.

The sky was an indigo blue, with a brilliant sun that poured down in hot waves. It has never been anything but a beautiful day when we've visited, I wondered, if it was by design.

I watched as Pax and Nessi went about picking up sticks, measuring them to ensure they were the right length. Nessi's, laughter was infectious and the happiness radiating from her was intoxicating. It was moments like these that made me wonder how I could have ever been angry with Pax and Vanessa for giving me the best gift of all. For allowing me to experience a joy I thought I never would.

Last year I'd read about two British scientists, Patrick Steptoe and Robert Edwards, who for the first time ever successfully managed to help a woman conceived through in-vitro fertilization. The baby, who was apparently thriving, was due mid-summer. I was now past my childbearing years, but science was making strides in the field of infertility, and as much as I loved Nessi I wouldn't have hesitated one last attempt—or two, or three. Pax however wouldn't have been so willing.

Not because of Nessi, but because our losses had left him emotionally drained, broken and traumatised, and fearful for my health, and wellbeing. That, I supposed, was the inherent difference between men and women. Women wouldn't think twice about risking their lives for that chance to feel life in them—it's our inherent nature.

"I'm getting old. I can't keep up with her." Pax wiped the film of sweat off his face with his hands and dried them on his jeans.

"Don't feel bad. At seven, she has boundless energy." I watched a squirrel making its way down a maple before hitting grass and setting the dogs into a frantic chase.

"Daddy, make Doodle and Noodle stop. They're going to hurt the squirrel." Nessi squealed, chasing after the yapping terrier and the floundering pug who was simply mimicking his brother.

"No, he won't, Baby. The squirrel will outrun them," Pax said, meeting Nessi's smile when his comment proved true.

"Come, Baby. Come lay your flowers down." I handed her the daisies.

Nessi counted them. "Nine daisies. This year we brought her nine daisies."

"That's right, Baby, one for every year of your birthday. You know what to do with them."

Pax and I watched Nessi set them in the vase then, touch her hand to her lips with a kiss aimed at Vanessa's tombstone just as we taught her to do. "Mommy, does your friend Vanessa know we visit her and that I bring her flowers all the time?"

"She does. She watches us from heaven."

"So, if she's in heaven I'll never get to meet her?"

"No, you won't, but when you're a bit older, Daddy and I are going to tell you all about her."

"All right, Mommy." She flashed me that beautiful smile that always made my world a wonderful and magical place.

Coming Soon

Visit our website at www.mllexi.com

Visit our blog at mllexi.blog

Author contact: mllexiauthor@gmail.com

Made in the USA
Columbia, SC
17 September 2018